"Get down! Get down!" Chandler hit the gas as more gunshots peppered the back window.

Bristol's knees dug into the floorboard as she leaned across the passenger seat, her hands covering her head. Glass continued to rain down on her. She tried to make herself as small as possible.

"Where are the shots coming from?" she shouted. "Was he beside the road or in the truck?"

Chandler glanced in his rearview mirror and removed a gun from his holster.

"No. You can't shoot. Spencer is with him." The thought of her son being shot, or the driver losing control and crashing, scared her to death.

He flashed her a quick look. "I don't see the boy."

"He's in that truck. I heard him yelling. Please don't take the chance."

The deputy eased off the accelerator. "The shooter was in the truck, but I don't see him behind us now. I need to call this in."

As Bristol listened to Chandler tell the dispatcher their location and repeat the description of the vehicle, her mind struggled with Rex being dead. If so, who had taken Spencer, and why?

Connie Queen has spent her life in Texas, where she met and married her high school sweetheart. Together they've raised eight children and are enjoying their grandchildren. Today, as an empty nester, Connie lives with her husband and her Great Dane, Nash, and is working on her next suspense novel.

Books by Connie Queen

Love Inspired Suspense

Justice Undercover
Texas Christmas Revenge
Canyon Survival
Abduction Cold Case
Tracking the Tiny Target

Visit the Author Profile page at LoveInspired.com.

TRACKING THE TINY TARGET

CONNIE QUEEN

LOVE INSPIRED SUSPENSE
INSPIRATIONAL ROMANCE

LOVE INSPIRED® SUSPENSE
INSPIRATIONAL ROMANCE

Recycling programs
for this product may
not exist in your area.

ISBN-13: 978-1-335-58777-0

Tracking the Tiny Target

For questions and comments about the quality of this book, please contact us
at CustomerService@Harlequin.com.

Love Inspired
22 Adelaide St. West, 41st Floor
Toronto, Ontario M5H 4E3, Canada
www.LoveInspired.com

Printed in U.S.A.

I can do all things through Christ which strengtheneth me.
—*Philippians* 4:13

I'd like to dedicate this book to my grandkids. I love that some of you are old enough to read them. Annabelle, Ainsley, CJ, Zachary, Gracie, Ben, Johnny, J, Jammer, Josiah, Jimena, Arabelle, Blaire, Leti, Carter, Allanah, Tatum, Hallie Ann and the ones that are yet to come.

ONE

Please, Lord, keep my little boy safe until I can get to him.

Even as Bristol Delaney silently uttered the prayer for the tenth time, her heart squeezed, making her breath labored and painful.

Fog lifted from the wet pavement, creating a white sheet of mist that made it difficult to see. Her front passenger tire hit a pothole, which caused her car to jerk to the right and off the pavement. The front end slid sideways before finding traction again. She eased off the accelerator and rounded the sharp curve.

Swirling emergency lights flashed before her eyes.

Cars and trucks lined both sides of the rural Texas highway. People stood in the ditch and some in the road, but Bristol didn't process the other parents and bystanders.

The lime-green daycare van, dotted with colorful painted handprint decals, came into view. She gasped. Even though the daycare director had called to tell her the van had been in an accident, Bristol hadn't expected it to be leaning against the steep incline—almost on its side, with the back end of the vehicle caved in. Two side windows were shattered, and the front door where the kids entered and exited stood ajar and twisted in a mangled mess.

It was much worse than she'd imagined.

Several of the daycare children, including her three-year-old son, attended a local preschool academy until eleven o'clock. Then Mr. Hewitt would pick them up and deliver them to Tender Tots Daycare, where they'd be served lunch, take a nap and spend the rest of their day.

What had Mr. Hewitt been thinking to take the daycare van this far off the normal route?

But even as Bristol's mind scrambled with the question, she knew the answer. The elderly driver probably had no choice. Something must've left him with no alternative.

Somehow, her ex-husband, Rex, had found her. But how? Had he escaped from prison?

No matter what Bristol had done to hide her tracks—from cutting ties with everyone from the previous town, including her coworkers, to avoiding social media—she'd failed.

If you think what happened to Mia was bad, it'll be nothing compared to what I have in store for you, sweetheart. Don't ever cross me.

After four years, Bristol Delaney could still feel her ex-husband's strong fingers clamped to her jaw, squeezing tighter and tighter. Despite intense pain, she'd refused to give him the satisfaction of crying out. The smell of cigarettes was suffocating as Rex's hot breath voiced his threat. Mia, his first wife, had been missing for years. Whatever happened to her couldn't be good. Was she even still alive?

She clutched the nine-millimeter Smith & Wesson to her chest while her other hand gripped the steering wheel ever tighter, fighting to keep her car on the rural highway. She'd do what it took to protect herself.

Instead of stopping, she continued through the maze of people at a turtle's pace.

A sheriff's deputy waved her through.

On the driver's side of the van, an older-model two-door pickup sat with the hood and front bumper crumpled. It was obvious to even the untrained eye the truck had rammed the van.

Tears pooled in her eyes. She braked as she drew alongside the wreckage, pulled into the opposite ditch, shoved her gun into her waistband and tugged her blouse over it. She jumped out of her car and darted across the road.

A deputy in a cowboy hat grabbed her before she could approach the van. "Ma'am, you can't go any farther."

"My son was in that van!" Even though she'd learned to school her emotions, tears ran freely, blinding her. She tried to jerk free. "Let me go."

"You'll have to stay behind that yellow tape." His grip remained firm, and sympathy lined his features as he pointed to the barrier some twenty yards away with a mob of people behind it. "This is being treated as a crime scene, and we can't allow anyone to contaminate the site."

It was then she noticed the body lying on the grass a few feet away from the bus, circled by a group of paramedics. *Mr. Hewitt.* A muscular paramedic was performing chest compressions. Her heart continued to pound out of control. Why hurt the van driver? The older man was a kind soul that enjoyed working with kids after his retirement.

"You need to move your vehicle out of the way so

emergency vehicles can access the scene, and then you may go stand with the rest of the families. We'll let you know as soon as we learn the whereabouts of the children."

That wasn't good enough. She couldn't sit by and wait while her boy might be getting farther away, but she kept the thought to herself. No one knew better than she did how dangerous Rex could be.

A dog barked. Deputies wearing black vests gathered in a circle, evidently ready to search for the children. A bloodhound waited patiently on his leash.

With long strides, she ran back to her car. But instead of pulling alongside the other vehicles, she continued down the highway several hundred yards and over a hill before parking in the ditch. The accident scene was out of sight. She had no intentions of messing up their investigation, but she had to find Spencer.

He was the only person she had in her life. She couldn't lose him. Ever.

She stepped out of the car, her running shoes disappearing into tall weeds, and then hiked up the steep incline onto solid forest ground. An old barbed-wire fence lay in front of her, and she quickly crossed it.

Secluded landscape lay out before her, and it was eerily quiet compared to the mob surrounding the wrecked daycare van. Bristol trekked through the dense woods, brushing away vines and thistles with her arm.

The authorities probably wouldn't be happy if they knew she'd gone out on her own. But if her ex-husband had taken Spencer and gotten a head start, she'd never see her son again.

No trails were laid out before her, and unless the driver of the truck had an accomplice who'd picked them up on the highway, Rex would've headed into the woods. He was an expert hiker and used to spend days on end camping in state parks. As she stepped over a fallen tree trunk, her gaze lit on a tiny footprint.

Bristol bent over and looked for more signs. At least three different imprints could be seen, but she didn't know if the diagonal markings belonged to Spencer's shoes. Who looked at the soles of their child's shoes?

Besides the child-size footprints, she also saw a large imprint, like that of a man's hiking boot. She put her running shoe in the impression and noticed how her foot was dwarfed compared to the one she stood in. Rex was over six feet tall and wore a size twelve.

Again, the sinking feeling this was Rex's doing consumed her. She removed the Smith & Wesson from her waistband and gripped it tightly, ready to use it if necessary. After fleeing her husband four years ago, one of the first things she'd done was buy the pistol and take a gun safety class.

As she continued through the brush, she tried to recall what her son had said about the other children. Four girls and two boys? Bristol couldn't be certain, but maybe it would help her if more shoe prints appeared.

Birds chirped on the limbs above, and a squirrel darted up the trunk of a tree. She listened for the sound of children's voices or cries but heard nothing. How long had they been out here? Surely no one could have gone far with six kids.

The trail dipped as the ground slowly declined. Late-May thunderstorms had been active the past two weeks, creating muddy puddles. Her gaze landed on more small footprints, and she followed them.

No doubt the kids were scared to death. She couldn't even imagine the terror they were feeling, surviving a wreck and then being brought out into the middle of nowhere.

If Rex was the one who'd taken the children, what were his plans? The truck was disabled. Did he have a secret location all planned out? An accomplice to pick him up? Would he hurt the kids so they couldn't talk? So many questions and no answers. She just had to keep searching and trust God to protect them.

Barking came from behind her in the distance. The rescue workers must be spreading out in the woods. She double-checked the pistol again to make certain the thumb safety was on and continued through the trees.

The faint cry of a child carried with the breeze. She stopped and listened. The sound came more from the right, toward the east. Careful not to make a noise, she took a step, hunkered low and picked her way through the brush, keeping an eye out for sticks that might snap. One calculated step at a time, she moved toward the source.

Occasionally, a footprint marked the way the children had gone. The brush grew thinner, and the ground again went downhill. Not knowing she'd be traipsing through the woods, she had worn a hot-pink T-shirt. Not exactly good camouflage attire.

Suddenly, movement caught her attention. A splash of color among the foliage, and her breath hitched.

Several children were grouped together and sitting on the ground. If the abductor was in the area, she couldn't see him. The leaves and brush made it difficult to see clearly, but she began counting the kids. One. Two. Three. Four.

Four. They were all girls.

That couldn't be right. She counted again and still came up two short. If her memory were correct, both boys were missing. Or maybe there had only been five children in the van today and the director had been mistaken. But she had specifically said six. Even as Bristol took another step forward, and then another, the blood pumped through her ears as her gaze searched for Spencer.

She recognized two of the kids. There was Chelsea, an adorable red-haired little girl, and a blonde named Leila. The other two girls she'd seen before but didn't recall their names. Mason, Spencer's friend, was not there.

As she continued to survey the scene, her gaze finally latched on to Chelsea's hands, which were behind her back. Then the others. All of them had their hands tied together. Bristol's teeth ground against each other. How could someone do this? She couldn't see if the children's feet were tied together because they sat on the ground.

Temptation to rush to the girls and ask them what they knew was overwhelming, but Bristol stayed put. She might put not only herself in danger but also the kids.

Please, Lord, help me find my son.

Even as her mind uttered the prayer, she wondered why Spencer and Mason weren't with the other children. Maybe they were sitting nearby, like behind a tree or something, but were blocked from view.

A dog barked again.

If she was correct and Rex was the one who'd taken the children, he must've nabbed Spencer and was moving farther away. But why take the other boy?

He doesn't know what Spencer looks like.

The realization hit her hard. Rex must've only discovered he had a son but had not seen a picture. When she'd finally had enough of his violence and learned of his multiple affairs, she'd left him—a decision she hadn't taken lightly. Even though he'd been a terrible, controlling husband, he wouldn't tolerate her leaving him—his threats believable. It was after he'd planted drugs on her and she'd unknowingly smuggled them across the Mexican border into Texas that she'd realized she had to leave. A month after running, she discovered she was pregnant.

Surmising the searchers would rescue the girls in a few minutes, she decided to go around the children and not draw attention to herself. Bristol silently moved to the right, keeping her eyes on the ground and searching for more shoe prints. Rex would've gone in the opposite direction of the wreck site.

A tall wall of vines among the cedars rose above her, and she stepped to go around them.

Somewhere close by, a twig snapped. There was a blur of movement and then cold, sharp metal pressed into her throat.

Her heart stampeded out of control. The sharp blade kept her from screaming.

Hot breath pressed against her ear. "Don't move. I'd love nothing more than to slice your throat."

Rex? The male voice was low and raspy. It'd been years since she'd heard him speak, but she was fairly certain it was him.

Her gun. *Use the gun.*

As if he could read her thoughts, a powerful hand gripped her wrist and yanked her arm behind her. Fingers dug into her skin. "Drop it."

She leaned back, trying to ease the pain as the blade dug deeper. Tears pooled in her eyes. No. She had to defend herself. She wasn't weak. With a jerk, she tried to wrestle from his grasp, but the blade went deeper. Blood trickled down her neck.

She released her gun, allowing it to fall to the ground. Her breath came in pants, and nausea swirled in her gut at the sting of the cut. "Where—" The word came out as a squeak. "Where is Spencer?"

"He's not your concern anymore."

In all her nightmares concerning her ex-husband, it'd been her life she thought at risk. Absolute terror slammed into her as she realized her death didn't compare to the horror of losing her child.

And this madman knew it.

Jarvis County sheriff deputy Chandler Murphy drew a breath as his gaze landed on a camo-masked man dressed in a black T-shirt holding a knife against someone's neck. Long, scraggly hair peeked out from the balaclava. Chandler shoved the boy's baseball cap that he'd used to get the scent in the pocket of his handler vest and then slid his Glock from his holster. Why had someone run into the woods on their own? Even though he knew the parents were upset, they should know better than to go traipsing off on their own until the area was secure. This guy could ruin the entire operation.

Without taking his gaze from the scene, he flicked his hand up, giving Tucker the signal to sit. The bloodhound obeyed. The canine had done his job and led him close enough to the children where he could see them huddled together. Chandler didn't want Tucker to give their position away and put the kids in greater danger, so they had continued quietly on. He performed a quick survey of the area and saw no more children besides the girls huddled together he'd spotted a minute earlier, but this was not a good situation. Too many variables, and things could go wrong.

He stepped to the right to give himself a better position.

The man struggled with his captor, and something dropped to the ground. A gun? As they wrestled, he got a glimpse of blond hair spilling over a pink shoulder.

A woman. Tension rose within him. Not only were there six children—two of whom he hadn't spotted yet— no doubt scared and maybe hurt, but also a woman. What was she thinking, putting everyone in jeopardy?

Shoving his anger aside, he quickly moved closer, checked to make certain no children were in his crosshairs and positioned himself behind a tree. He couldn't take a chance on hitting the woman, so he took aim at the man and waited for his line of fire to clear. The man tugged the woman closer, his arm tightening around her neck, making the risk too great to shoot.

Chandler didn't think he'd been spotted and again went on the move. He stepped through the brush silently and patiently worked his way closer. The woman fought, jerking and kicking, trying to free herself. He prayed her actions didn't get her killed.

He closed the distance.

The woman squealed and repeatedly demanded, "Let me go."

"I'll slice your throat," the man bit out.

Crying sounded to the left. The children were close.

Either the woman was so intent on getting away she didn't hear the words or she didn't care, for she didn't cease kicking and clawing as they worked their way down the hill. One slip of her foot, and the man's knife could kill her. Chandler had to make his move before one of the kids wandered into the path of danger.

Hoping the woman's actions kept the man's attention, Chandler silently sprinted toward the two with his gun ready. Just as he reached them, the man turned toward him. Through the slit of the mask, their gazes locked.

In a flash, the man reared back and threw the knife, stabbing Chandler in his left shoulder. Pain shot through him, and he stutter-stepped, giving the man time to dart through the brush.

Chandler raised his Glock with his finger on the trigger, when a small girl stumbled into his peripheral vision. The child cried, "Mama! I want my mama."

As the masked man wove through the trees, he turned and gave Chandler one more look and then continued down the hill. Chandler watched until he disappeared and then dropped his gun to his side before holstering it.

A yell came from behind them. The other officers and rescuers were approaching.

The lady found her gun in the tall grass and turned in the direction the man had gone.

Chandler stepped toward her, holding his injured shoulder. "No. Stay here."

She looked at him, the blond hair blowing away from her face, her blue eyes slamming into his. "He has my son."

Chandler's lungs froze. "Bristol Delaney?" Bristol was Rex Edwards's ex-wife—the woman Chandler had repeatedly tried to find so he could question her about Rex's probable connection in his dad's murder. She had waltzed into the station and "anonymously" turned evidence against her drug-dealing husband and then disappeared. Since officially Chandler wasn't supposed to know about her involvement, he had to keep his inquiry under wraps. The woman had successfully managed to elude Chandler for years. "Stay right there. That man's dangerous."

"He has my son," she repeated and turned to run.

Reaching out, Chandler lunged for her. She slid out of his grasp and headed deeper into the woods. He'd been trying to find his dad's killer for years. She wasn't going to get away from him this time.

He got to his feet and ran after her.

TWO

Bristol darted through the trees while keeping an eye on her target. She knew Chandler Murphy—the deputy who'd kept trying to get ahold of her after she'd left town in the middle of the night—would not be happy. But if Rex got away, she might never see her son again. A chance she wasn't willing to take.

The masked man disappeared over the next hill, and she slowed to a jog, not wanting to run up on him. He'd thrown a knife, but he could also have a gun or another weapon. Her own nine-millimeter was still in her grip.

Where was Spencer? Had Rex hidden him in the foliage?

As she topped the rise, she saw nothing but trees and forests. She paused and quickly glanced around.

A blur of movement to the left nabbed her attention. She waited and watched. Whatever was down there wasn't big. Spencer?

She took off at a run, when something grabbed her by the back of the shirt and stopped her in her tracks. The nine-millimeter slipped in her hand, and she juggled with it until she regained control.

"Stay where you are." Chandler.

"Let go of me." She yanked free of his grip, but he

moved closer and captured her bicep, spinning her around until she was staring into his hazel eyes.

"Be still," he whispered. "You're going to get somebody killed. Is that your boy?"

She looked back and zeroed in on the crying child about thirty yards from them. A blond-haired boy dressed in a red shirt and jeans.

Realization crashed into her, making her throat constrict. It wasn't Spencer. "No. That's Mason Calloway. Now let me go."

"Promise to be quiet and not run off again. I could have you arrested for interfering with an active apprehension."

"You wouldn't dare." She kept her voice down but caught the challenge in his expression. He might. Irritation crawled all over her. Her ex had bullied her for years, and no doubt Chandler believed she would cower before him. He was mistaken if he thought she'd shy away.

"Let me do my job. The children's safety is my first priority."

"Mine, too." She yanked her arm out of his hands. Physically, she was no match for the brawny man, but there were other ways to control a situation.

Chandler put his mouth close to her ear. "Tucker, my bloodhound, is going to track the assailant."

She glanced over her shoulder. "Will the dog hurt my boy?"

"No. He's trained for search and rescue, not to attack." He looked at her. "I need you to go back with the other parents. You'll be notified when we find your son."

She shook her head. If being married to Rex had taught her anything, it was that she controlled her own destiny. "Not happening. You don't know who you're dealing with. If Rex has Spencer, I'll never see my boy again."

"I'm familiar with Rex. I'm certain you're aware of that." He held his shoulder with his other hand, and she noticed blood seeped through his polo shirt. She cringed.

"Are you okay?"

"Fine. It's not deep."

Bristol drew a deep breath. Investigators from the sheriff's department had left messages on her voice mail trying to get in touch with her after she turned in Rex for drug smuggling to the police. The police had told Bristol her name would remain anonymous, and she didn't know how word had gotten out. But she was determined not to say anything more. She had taken a big chance by turning in her husband and didn't plan on drawing any more attention from him or his friends. She'd hoped never to see Rex again.

Bristol had changed cell phone numbers and found a new place to live outside Liberty, Texas. The only person she gave her new number to when she left was Rachel Whitson, a widow with three children who'd noticed bruises Rex had left on her arm. Rachel had been like a second mom and had introduced her to God. The widow called Bristol to let her know Chandler had phoned twice trying to locate her.

"You believe Rex had something to do with your dad's disappearance?"

His jaw twitched, and emotion sizzled in his hazel eyes. "Yes." He swallowed. "But we don't know if Rex Edwards is the man who has your son. Right now, I'm going to treat this like any other case. Safety precautions and all."

Temptation to argue tugged at her, but she swallowed down a retort. "Okay. If I stay back, can I go with you?"

He shook his head. "I can't have you interfering."

"I won't."

His lips pressed together in a slight grimace. "I don't like this, but if you come with me, you must promise you'll do as I say."

"Okay."

"Say the words."

She looked at him. Time was wasting, and she didn't pretend not to understand. "I promise to do as you say."

He nodded. "Good."

Chandler's two-way radio crackled to life, and a lady's voice came over the airwaves. "We found four girls. All are safe."

He pushed the mic. "Ten-four, Hattie. There are still two more children missing, both boys. The perpetrator is armed and on the run with one boy. The other child's hands are tied, and he's dressed in jeans. He's about one hundred yards due north of the girls."

"We have the boy in sight," Hattie informed him. "Will be there in two minutes."

"In pursuit of the suspect and the other boy."

"Ten-four."

He shot Bristol a glance before grabbing the harness of his bloodhound, who'd been standing quietly by. "Ready, Tucker." He placed the boy's cap in front of the dog's nose. "Search."

That was Spencer's favorite cap, with the tractor on it. A lump formed in her throat. Her little boy loved tractors and played with them all the time. She'd bought him the hat nearly a year ago, and the boy wore it every chance he got, but she'd asked him not to bring it to daycare for fear it'd get lost or ruined. He must've sneaked it into his backpack today.

The dog took off down the hill at a run, his tail pointed at attention, as Chandler held on to his leash.

Bristol stayed on the deputy's heels but allowed enough distance she wouldn't ram him if he came to an abrupt halt. The incline grew steep as they neared the bottom of the hill, causing her shoe to slip in the mud. Her hand automatically shot out and grabbed the back of Chandler's black safety vest for balance. She pulled him to a stop and regained her balance. "Sorry."

"You okay?"

"Yeah."

He took off again with her following. The brush and vines thickened, forcing them to slow to a walk. A narrow creek snaked across the valley floor. Tucker leaped across, taking Chandler with him. Bristol jumped, but her running shoe landed in the water, soaking her foot past the ankle.

Tucker kept his nose to the ground and sniffed before tugging against the leash again. Bristol knew little about search-and-rescue dogs, but the bloodhound appeared to be more excited as he wove his way through the dense foliage. Like the scent had grown stronger.

Boom!

The gunshot made Bristol jump, and her heart leaped into her throat.

Chandler stopped and put his hand in the air. Wispy limbs and briars encased them, making it impossible to see outside their thicket cave. He turned to her and mouthed, "Don't move."

In one swift motion, he signaled for Tucker to lie down. The bloodhound obeyed.

Her heart continued to stampede as she strained to

listen. It was impossible to tell if the noises in the woods were caused by the squirrels scattering for shelter and the breeze in the trees or if Rex was on the move.

A tiny cry rose above the wind, and she froze. She'd recognize Spencer's cry anywhere. Her motherly instinct to race to her son flowed through her very being, but Chandler grabbed her arm. He repeated, "Don't move."

"Mommy!"

Spencer's scream sent chills down her spine. She jerked her arm. "I can't. I have to save him."

Chandler's grip tightened. "Don't do it. You'll get the boy hurt."

Angry, panicked tears pooled in her eyes, blinding her. With her arm still in his grasp, she took a step into the brush.

Another shot rang out.

"Get down." Chandler noted the terror in her eyes, but he didn't dare let her go. He pushed her to the ground. "Keep your head down."

She bent at the knees, resting on her haunches, but stared into the brush.

"Deputies should be on their way. This guy is on foot. He can't get far. Don't jeopardize your boy's safety."

She blinked, as if conflicted, then shot him a glare.

His heart went out to her, but he could not—would not—allow her to compromise the situation. The sheriff would have his badge if he allowed Bristol or her son to get hurt when he should have demanded she wait with the others.

If it hadn't been for him being just as eager to catch his father's killer, he might have taken the time to secure Bristol with another deputy. But he also wasn't certain which side of the law she stood on. Even though she'd turned evidence against her husband, she had admitted to transporting drugs across the border—knowledge that Chandler wasn't supposed to be privy to. Word had gotten around the department anyhow. Was she innocent, or had she only told on Rex because she'd wanted out of the marriage?

Chandler's father, Simon Murphy, had been surveilling Rex Edwards for weeks when he didn't come home one night. His truck had been found abandoned on the side of the highway, but there had been no sign of his dad. A year later, Rex had been sentenced to five years for dealing drugs, but the man also deserved to pay for his father's murder if he was responsible. And apparently, like so many others, the man hadn't served his full sentence but had been let out early.

Chandler's mom had begged Chandler to quit his career with the sheriff's department after his dad's disappearance, but he hadn't listened. How could he rest until someone paid for what they did?

His shirt stuck to the stab wound, and it smarted when the cloth pulled free. At least the bleeding had almost stopped.

"Do you have a plan?"

He put his finger to his lips and whispered, "We wait for backup."

Her eyes squinted in a scowl, telling him she wasn't happy with his strategy. But he needed to catch this guy while keeping her safe. Nothing fancy. Just do his job. He wouldn't fail his dad again.

A twig snapped. Then more sobbing from the child.

The sounds grew closer. Was the guy purposely coming their way instead of trying to get away? Or was he uncertain of his and Bristol's location and didn't realize he was coming right for them? He motioned for Bristol to get under a bush as he readied his Glock. Silently, he climbed to his feet while still hunkering low. His gaze searched out their surroundings, but he didn't see their man.

Footsteps drew nearer.

Suddenly, the guy came into view about ten yards away. He still wore his mask and held the boy by the shirt collar. Chandler had familiarized himself with Rex Edwards, and the masked man had the same six-foot-two build and looked to weigh about 220 pounds. But he couldn't be certain if the man was Rex with his face hidden by the mask.

Tears rolled down the boy's face, and his cheeks burned red.

Chandler's jaw twitched as he tamped down his anger. He took a quick glance, hoping to see other deputies moving in, but saw no one.

"I want my mama." The boy's lips puckered, and his eyebrows drew in.

"I told you to keep your mouth shut." The man shook him. "I won't tell you again."

Spencer's frown deepened.

Tucker's ears perked, and he cocked his head. Before Chandler could give him the signal to remain quiet, the bloodhound let out a sharp yelp.

The masked man's head jerked toward the tiny thicket cave. Leaves camouflaged the view, but their eyes found each other. The man grew still, and he stared at Chandler.

Chandler took aim, and his finger tightened on the trigger.

"That was a dog!" Spencer cried. He went into a

frenzy, jerking against the man's grasp and slapping at the guy's hand. "Let me go."

Fear that he might accidentally shoot the boy kept Chandler from pulling the trigger.

"I'm a deputy with Jarvis County Sheriff's Department. Let the boy go," he called out. "I've got you covered. Deputies have saturated the woods. There's no escape."

The guy pulled the boy in front of his chest. "Oh, I will escape, Deputy Murphy." He said the name with emphasis to show Chandler he knew who he was. "I'm taking the brat with me. And if you've got his mama with you, ask her why she ever got involved with someone like Rex Edwards. She transported drugs across the border from Mexico and was a user herself. Don't let her convince you she's an innocent victim. Pay attention to how she's always sleepy, irritable and never has money. Classic signs of a user. And then you tell her she'll pay, like Mia, for keeping the boy from his daddy."

Before Chandler could react, the masked man fired three quick shots into the brush. Bullets ricocheted against the limbs and trees. He ducked.

The boy screamed as they took off in the opposite direction.

"Are you all right?" Chandler glanced down at Bristol, her eyes dancing with fear. At her nod, he took off after the man and the boy with Tucker leading the way.

Careful not to run up on them, he kept a tight rein on Tucker's leash as they snaked through the dense vegetation. Within a few minutes, he'd lost their trail. A rustle sounded behind him. He turned to see Bristol searching the brush, and about twenty yards behind her, two of his fellow deputies.

"Watch her," he told the deputies. He gave Tucker his

lead. They couldn't afford to lose the boy now. Finally, he let go of the leash, and the bloodhound put his nose to the ground. He barked and veered to the right. After crossing a narrow creek, Tucker sniffed the boy's baseball cap again. But Chandler could tell he hadn't found the scent yet. A couple of minutes later, the other deputies caught up to him.

Deputy Green asked, "Did you lose the trail?"

"I'm afraid so."

Bristol stepped up. "How could you lose them? I purposely stayed back so I wouldn't distract the dog."

"We'll catch him. There's three of us." He turned to Deputy Green. "Make certain she makes it back to the others."

"No way." She shook her head. "My boy is in danger." An engine revved.

He and Bristol looked at each other before Chandler took off at a run.

Tucker beat the ground at a full-out sprint, and Chandler followed him through the trees. The sounds of a vehicle faded away.

The woods ended at a highway. A white-haired man in jeans and a worn cowboy hat stared at him as he approached. The older man shoved his hat back and rubbed his forehead. A trickle of blood ran down the side of his face.

A blur of blue disappeared around a curve on a hill.

Panting for breath, Chandler asked, "Are you okay?"

The man squinted against the pain. "Yeah. That jerk hit me in the head and took my truck."

He turned as Bristol and the deputies caught up to him.

Chandler asked the older man, "What happened?"

"This masked guy came running out of the woods

waving his hands like he was mad. If he hadn't had the boy with him, I probably wouldn't have stopped. As soon as I pulled over, he jerked open my door and sucker punched me in the jaw." He shook his fist.

"What kind of truck do you own?"

"Blue 2002 Ford F-150 extended cab. Has an I'd Rather Be Fishing bumper sticker in the back window."

"Thanks." Chandler pressed his mic. "Suspect is headed northwest on FM 51. A mile or so north of the wreckage." He gave a description of the truck.

Deputy Hattie Perkins said, "Ten-four. Deputy Andrews is en route."

Tucker sniffed tire tracks on the pavement where the suspect's and Spencer's scents disappeared.

The victim's injury had already stopped bleeding. "Do you need medical care?" Chandler asked.

"Nah. I'm good."

He hit the mic again. "Can you send a cruiser after us?"

"There's no one else, but I can do it. Be there shortly."

Bristol started marching on the highway the way the vehicle had gone.

"Can you take pics of these?" Chandler pointed to the tracks in the mud. "And get the rest of the information from our witness?"

Deputy Green said, "Already on it."

He trusted Green to secure the scene and collect the evidence they needed, even if there wasn't much. A BOLO came over the airway for a blue truck and gave the vicinity. It could be an advantage there wasn't much traffic on the back roads, especially at the noon hour. Bad news was the closest town with a police department was fifteen miles away, so except for the deputies working the crash site, there were no officers nearby.

Chandler ran to catch up with Bristol. He started to tell her just to wait for Deputy Perkins, but he knew she wouldn't listen. She needed to keep moving and feel like she was doing something to find her son. He'd felt the same need when his father had disappeared five years ago. Fear and determination radiated off her. If Rex Edwards was the one who'd grabbed her son, he agreed the boy was in danger. But they didn't know he was the suspect for certain.

The man could be a relative or a friend of Rex. Or no connection to her ex but rather a random child abduction. They needed to be sure of the abductor's identity.

Chandler's eyebrows rose. "Was it Rex?"

"What?" she snapped.

"You heard the kidnapper's voice. Was it your ex-husband?"

"Yes. I…" She frowned. "I can't be certain. It sounded like him. But maybe different."

Chandler was familiar with the man but had never spoken with him personally.

A couple of minutes later, Deputy Hattie Perkins came around the corner in her crew-cab truck. He and Bristol climbed into the back seat, and Tucker sat between them.

"Where to?" Deputy Perkins asked.

"Follow this road."

She glanced in her rearview mirror at him. Normally, Chandler would've taken the time to go back for his truck, but he wanted to check out Abbeytown, the next community over.

Bristol stared out the side window, probably looking for the blue truck. This area was about twenty minutes on the outskirts of Liberty. Small towns were scattered throughout the countryside between farms and ranches, some only with a row of houses and maybe a gas station or grain elevator. Rock roads splintered off the highway. Chandler was familiar with the area, but there were literally hundreds of places to hide.

He kept watch out his side window. Minutes later, his cell phone rang. "This is Murphy."

"What's going on? I'm at the crash site. News journalists are all over this place."

Chandler drew a deep breath at Sheriff Carroll's voice. If there was one thing his boss disliked more than letting the suspect get away, it was trying to work a case with cameras rolling and microphones being shoved in his face. "Deputy Perkins and I are in pursuit of the suspect."

"Is our guy in sight?"

"No, sir. I only got a glimpse of a vehicle speeding away, but the owner of the stolen truck was at the scene."

"I need you to return here and help us sort through this mess and make certain we have everything from our witness."

Chandler had already talked with a witness to the bus crash—a fifty-five-year-old woman who was returning home from the post office when the daycare van flew up on her car, driving erratically. Then the van passed her on a curve, followed by a silver pickup that was riding the van's bumper. She'd been the first person to call 9-1-1 to complain about the reckless drivers and express concern for the children. "I'd like to ask permission to stay in pursuit of our suspect. There's a possibility the man is Rex Edwards."

"Edwards." Silence stretched out several seconds. "I didn't realize he was out of prison. What makes you think so?"

He didn't look at Bristol, although he could feel her

eyes on him. "His ex-wife is with me, and the missing male child is his son."

A whistle came across the channel. "Okay, proceed. But, Murphy, I don't have to remind you to go by the book."

"Yes, sir." He clicked off, and even though the sheriff didn't say it, Chandler knew his commander wouldn't want him jumping to conclusions and messing up the investigation. Chandler had every intention of crossing every *t* and dotting every *i*. He glanced at Bristol.

Blue eyes stared back. He couldn't tell what she was thinking, but he got the feeling she had little confidence in him. Not that he blamed her. Frustration had sat on Chandler ever since he'd failed to find his father's killer. Yes, his father's body was never found, but deep in his gut, Chandler knew he was dead. There was no way his dad could be alive after five years and not return to his family.

"Deputy Perkins, you can turn around. Take me back to my truck, please."

She glanced in the mirror at him. Without a word, the deputy turned the truck around on the next side road.

He shifted to Bristol. "And you can get back to your vehicle. If you'll give me your cell number, I'll call you as soon as we learn something."

"That's unnecessary." The words came out low and curt, and her lips pressed together.

His jaw twitched. He really didn't need the distraction right now. But he could see by her demeanor that she had no intention of going home.

THREE

Bristol's stomach twisted into knots, eager to get back to her car and find the blue truck. Every second that ticked off made her worry Spencer was getting farther away. Her poor little boy. He'd sounded so scared and confused in the woods. It'd taken everything in her power not to run to him.

Her heart constricted. What if she never found him? Lost forever, like Chandler had lost his dad, not knowing if he were alive or dead. Never to see him again or know if he was safe. She didn't think she could deal with that. Ever.

She hugged herself tight. *Please, God, keep Spencer safe until I find him. Lead me to him.*

The prayer made her feel somewhat better. Talking with God had helped get her through the fear after Rex had abused her, emotionally and physically. Even though she'd never been able to rely on other people, she'd found it easy to turn to God. But this was different. She could fight back, whereas Spencer had no chance on his own.

Deputy Perkins pulled into the ditch. The ambulance was gone, and a wrecker was being hooked up to the daycare van. The deputy said, "Looks like most of the paramedics are gone, except for Archie. Glad the sheriff's brother was here. Probably saved the van driver's life."

Bristol asked, "Do they think Mr. Hewitt will make it?"

The female deputy nodded. "He was breathing on his own when they left for the hospital, so it looks promising." She glanced at Chandler and pointed to his shoulder. "You need medical care for that wound."

"I'll be fine," Chandler mumbled. "I have a first aid kit in my truck."

Deputy Perkins frowned. "Whatever. The sheriff won't be happy when it gets infected and you have to miss work."

Bristol agreed with Deputy Perkins and figured Chandler could use a few stitches, but evidently, he was stubborn.

A truck with a Jarvis County Sheriff's Department emblem sat in the middle of all the activity. Several people milled around, and Bristol caught sight of Mason Calloway. The boy rested securely in the arms of a nice-looking guy wearing slacks and a dress shirt. She recognized Rebecca Calloway beside the man, an infant cradled in her arms. With her free hand, Rebecca ran her fingers through Mason's hair.

A lump formed in Bristol's throat. She was happy for the family, truly she was, but a spot of jealousy tugged at her. At this moment, she'd do anything to have her little family of two reunited.

Bristol climbed out of the truck and avoided the few other parents who still lingered with their children. A deputy visited with a lady with a little girl Bristol recognized from the group. The girl clung desperately to the woman Bristol assumed was her mom.

Instead of waiting to be interviewed, Bristol headed for her car.

"Bristol, wait up."

She didn't slow at Chandler's voice.

"Come on. Don't do this."

She spun on her heel and faced the deputy. "You can't stop me from looking for my boy."

Frustration bit at his expression, but then he quickly reined it in. "I realize that. But I also can't have you getting in my way."

"Point made." She saluted him and strode to her car. After she got in, she pulled onto the highway and glimpsed Chandler in her rearview mirror staring after her, his arms folded across his massive chest and the bloodhound at his side.

Since they'd already driven on this highway for several miles, she took the first left past the road where Rex had stolen the truck. No doubt he wouldn't want to be caught and would move out of the county as fast as possible.

The last prison Rex had been in was the Roach Unit in West Texas. Terrible name for a prison, if you asked her—not that there were any good ones. Incarcerated people's basic information was available online, and research told her a lot of inmates got moved to Huntsville, near Houston, before getting released. She'd been so busy studying for finals so she could obtain her teaching certificate that she hadn't looked up Rex's information this whole semester. How could she have been so careless?

The road dead-ended into Lover's Leap Lane—a narrow rock road. Indecision plagued her. Would Rex take a route like this because it would be less traveled, or stick to the pavement so he could move faster?

Still uncertain, she sighed and turned onto Lover's Leap, crossed a wooden bridge and passed several pastures of cattle. Not a single farmhouse in sight. To put up a front for his drug dealing, Rex had worked as a plant manager for a concrete company during the day and dealt drugs at night. Before he got into management, he'd been a cement truck driver. No doubt he'd learned the area like the back of his hand during his driving days.

She transported drugs across the border... That someone would think she'd taken part in smuggling, even if unknowingly, infuriated her. If there were any doubt the kidnapper was Rex, it had vanished with the masked man's words. Besides a couple of detectives, Rex was the only person who knew of her incident moving drugs across the border—since it was his fault. Her ex-husband had given her a pricey leather swing coat, and she carried it with her from Del Rio on the border of Mexico home to North Texas in her suitcase. When they'd crossed the border, the agents had searched their car, and the drug-sniffing dogs alerted. But a box van gained the agents' attention, and they'd let Rex and her go. At the time, she had thought the search routine.

The quality of the coat had impressed Bristol, and she'd even noticed how heavy it felt. When she went to hang it in the closet, a small bag filled with white powder fell to the floor. As silly as it was, her first thought was to wonder why someone had dropped confectioners' sugar in her coat. Then realization dawned. Drugs. Sixty tiny bags had been sewn into the lining. She'd been so upset with Rex for using her, but, more important, she'd been furious with herself and wondered how she could be so naive. She'd been a fool.

If law enforcement had found the fentanyl—the drug

had been identified later—she would've been left holding the bag—literally. But Rex had trusted Bristol to look cute and maybe even a little classy. Anything but a drug smuggler. He'd even admitted that to her when confronted. Her trust had made her the perfect patsy.

Despite the violence Rex would enact on her should he learn of her plan, she'd hid five bags of the deadly poison from the coat in an old pair of cowboy boots she kept on the top shelf in their closet. It took her a full three weeks after that day to gather the courage to anonymously call the sheriff's department with her information. If they could guarantee her identity would remain secret, she would turn in the bags of fentanyl and inform them of Rex's next drop and the names of his known contacts. For her cooperation, they'd promised her identity would remain a secret and she would not be prosecuted for her part in transporting the drugs.

She'd sneaked out at 3:00 a.m. with only a suitcase in her possession and had never looked back.

A curve appeared up ahead, and the pastures turned into a wooded area. She was thankful she'd let off the accelerator, because a golden retriever lay by the road near a driveway. She hit the brakes, barely missing the dog. She mumbled, "Watch out."

The retriever got up and jogged to the side of her car with his tongue hanging out and his tail wagging.

With a glance down the driveway, she noticed an old farmhouse with a wraparound porch and a variety of barns and sheds scattered about the property. She surveyed the place, searching for a blue truck, but couldn't see any vehicles for all the trees. Should she check the place out?

Why not? If she spotted the truck, she could always call Chandler. She grabbed her cell phone from the passenger seat and slid it under her leg. A tug on her shirt exposed her gun in its holster. Quick access could mean the difference between life and death. She turned into the drive and meandered down the long gravel path, keeping alert for any movement.

The dog trotted beside her car, seemingly happy to have a visitor. As she neared the home, she slowed to a stop, glanced around and then eased forward again. Mentally, she prepared herself for a speedy escape.

Birds flew from the power lines to the trees, and the golden retriever jogged to the front porch and barked. Everything appeared calm. She stopped in front of the house. Still no vehicles in sight, but the drive continued around the back. She sighed. She hated to invade someone's property, especially if Rex had not stopped by here. Chances were, he hadn't. And going to the front door put distance between her and her car, a chance she wasn't willing to take.

Proceeding around back, she glimpsed a man in his fifties wearing jeans and a Western shirt. He stood beside a tractor parked under a shade tree, and an open toolbox lay on the ground.

She rolled down her window as he approached.

"Can I help you?"

"I was looking for a blue truck and thought it might've come by here."

He looked perplexed, like he'd expected her to be lost.

Now that she had said the words, she realized the likelihood of her picking the right house was almost zilch. The man probably thought her silly.

"Haven't seen anyone like that here." Oddly, his eyes bored into hers.

"All right. I appreciate it. Did you see anyone drive by this way about thirty minutes ago?"

"No, ma'am. Already told you, the man ain't here. You be on about your way." He flicked his hand at her in a shooing motion.

The dog appeared beside her car and eagerly wagged his tail.

The man's rudeness surprised her. She realized he was probably busy working on his tractor, but most people in the country tended to be friendlier. Especially men to a woman—the old treat-her-as-a-lady thing. She shot him a fake smile before turning her car around in the drive.

One last glance at the man showed him returning to his farm equipment, and the dog ambled beside him.

Ruff. Ruff. The dog's hackles rose as he stared toward the shed.

Her window was still down, and she heard the man snap, "Get back here, Dolly!"

With her gaze on the review mirror, she eased up the drive. The man slapped his thigh and again commanded the dog to return. A bad feeling came over her. Something was wrong.

Already told you, the man ain't here. But she hadn't told him it was a man in the truck. She'd asked if anyone had driven by.

Was someone there? If so, why had the dog greeted her at the end of the driveway? In Bristol's experience, dogs normally only did that when they followed someone out of the drive. Had someone left?

What to do now? If Rex was there, she might cause him to panic and hurt Spencer. Or the farmer.

Maybe she should call Chandler. She hadn't even taken his number. As she came to the road, she turned left and pulled slightly off to the side, but the house was still in view. The trees blocked the man and the barns from sight, but at least she'd know if someone left the home.

Bristol was used to handling things on her own, especially after being married to Rex. She'd made herself vulnerable by believing in and depending on him. Even though her mom had tried to do what was best for Bristol—her only child—she'd never been able to provide a living, jumping from one romantic relationship to another. Much to her chagrin, Bristol had followed in her mom's steps by plunging into marriage with Rex. Was it possible being a poor judge of character was hereditary?

Chandler seemed to want to help her. Or maybe it was just that he believed Rex had killed his father. Either way, she wanted Spencer safe from her ex.

She was certain the sheriff's department could contact Chandler for her, but she'd probably have to explain the reason to the dispatcher first. He also worked for the Bring the Children Home Project, an organization that helped find missing children. Contacting them might be simpler. She quickly found their contact information and called the number.

"Bring the Children Home Project. This is Josie."

"Hello, Josie. Deputy Chandler Murphy is working the case of the wrecked daycare van. My son is the boy still missing. I need to contact the deputy."

"What's your name?"

"Bristol Delaney."

"Okay, I thought so. Chandler has updated us on the situation. I'll give you his number if you're ready."

"Ready."

Josie rattled off the number, and Bristol entered it into her phone.

"Thank you." After clicking off, she glanced back to the farmhouse, hesitant to call Chandler. What if she was wrong and the deputy was in the middle of pursuing a lead? There was no sign of the golden retriever or the farmer. Maybe she was mistaken, and the guy was just unfriendly.

Rex could be getting farther away while she sat here wasting time in her car. If only she could see what was going on.

She stepped out of her car with the cell phone in her hand and walked to the front of the vehicle, careful to stay out of sight. Branches blocked her view, so she moved closer to the driveway. She peeked around the trunk of a pecan tree, and the tractor came into view.

A breath released from her lungs. Rex wasn't there that she could see. If only the property owner had been more receptive, she could've asked where this road went or how many houses were on it. Anything to give her a hint of where to look or give her a sense if she was on the right track.

She turned to go back, when suddenly a dog yelped. Dolly?

A glance back showed two men struggling with each other. There *was* someone there!

She hurried to her car as she hit Chandler's number. Three rings and it went to voice mail. "This is Bristol. I need help. I think I found Rex." She drew a breath. What was the road? Her mind scrambled to remember. Finally, she recalled the name. "I'm on Lover's Leap Lane. The mailbox says Mabry."

A child's scream lifted on the wind.

"Spencer!"

* * *

Chandler continued to talk with Deputy Joyner, the investigator in the sheriff's department, as he sat in the parking lot of a closed feed store. Evidently, the businesses in Abbeytown that had once thrived couldn't stay afloat as more people left the farming world for city careers. Sheriff Carroll hadn't been in a good mood and demanded Chandler have his shoulder looked at.

Getting stitched up didn't take long, and he'd been happy to get away from the crash site. The sheriff's brother, Archie—Moose to most of the department, because of his large size—had been with paramedics and was still checking a couple of people out. Several journalists lingered, having no intention of leaving, probably hoping for breaking news.

The clicking of a keyboard sounded. "Edwards shows to be in the Roach Unit in Childress. That's odd. He should've been moved to Huntsville last week."

"Any property belonging to family or known acquaintances in this area?" Frustration bit at him. They weren't even certain the suspect was Rex Edwards. Was it possible Chandler wanted the kidnapper to be Rex? He had to keep an open mind.

"Not that I can find. But I'll keep looking because all I have is what was in the arrest records. Let me do some digging."

"Okay. Let me know if you learn anything." He clicked off. Deputy Joyner was a competent investigator, but it never hurt to have two people looking into the case. The first person he'd called was Josie Hunt, the investigator with Bring the Children Home Project who had also worked for the Liberty Police Department before going off on her own as a private detective. There were benefits to working with two organizations.

Except for Bristol, probably no one knew Edwards's past more than Chandler. Rex had been employed by the Warner Concrete Company for twelve years and had worked his way up to management before his arrest. Since he was still in jail, who was the masked man?

Did someone else have a reason to take Bristol's boy?

The masked man's words came back to him. *Classic signs of a user.* Did Bristol owe a dealer money? That was ridiculous. But what did he know about her? Nothing except that she'd turned evidence against her husband. What had made her get involved with Rex? Bristol wouldn't be the first person bamboozled by a love interest.

But still. Was it possible Bristol had something to hide? Or maybe someone was trying to use Spencer against her. After the trial that sent Rex to prison for dealing, Chandler had tried for weeks to find his wife—ex-wife—but she'd managed to evade him. Did she know more about his dealings than she had said?

His phone buzzed, and he glanced down to see the voice-mail light blinking. As Bristol's voice came across the line, claiming she might have found Rex, his throat constricted. Then a child's scream sounded in the background before the message abruptly ended.

He spun his truck around and headed toward Lover's Leap Lane, flying across the back roads.

Tucker whimpered from the back. The dog had an instinct for when they were going in on a case.

He'd known he shouldn't have let her go off by herself. Bristol wasn't in the right frame of mind to make logical decisions but was thrown into that motherly protective mode. Chandler had first witnessed the lengths a mom would go to when he was nine. While fishing with his mom, he'd started for the house to get a soda, when a bull got after him. Faster than a jackrabbit with his tail ablaze, his mom put herself between him and the massive animal. Thankfully, the bull didn't want any part of her. Later that night, his dad had half joked to him and his sister, Sydney, to never get between a mom and her child.

As Chandler slowed for a turn, he hit Bristol's number. No answer. Lover's Leap Lane appeared to his right, and he made the turn. Surprisingly, Bristol had called him as soon as she was in trouble. Doubt that she was the target or had had anything to do with Rex's drug deals made him hesitant to even consider the possibility. But, after years of working cases, Chandler had learned not everyone was as innocent as they seemed.

His truck bounced over the rocky road, sending up a huge white dust cloud billowing behind it. As he approached a curve in the road, he spotted the mailbox with the name Mabry and whipped into the drive. Bristol's car sat in the drive near the house. A glance around showed no others, but he continued cautiously toward the back of the modest home.

Ice ran through his veins as his gaze lit on her car as he went to go around. Deployed airbags dangled listlessly, and the front end was crumpled to half its size.

His boot hit the brake, and he jumped out of his truck and hurried to her vehicle. No one was inside. He turned and looked around.

Bristol yelled in a shaky voice, "Over here!"

She sat on the ground with an older man hunched over her. The blue Ford truck partially stuck out from behind the barn. Chandler strode their way. "What happened?"

Bristol stared into her hands. "He got away with Spencer, and he stole his truck." She jerked her thumb toward the farmer. An ugly bump marked her forehead, and her forearm was swelling with what looked like a long scrape.

"Let me see that arm."

She pulled away from his touch and cradled it with her other hand. "The airbag hit me, but I'm fine." Blue eyes gazed up at him. "Let's go get my son."

"Hold on, Bristol. I need to know what happened. Have you called in this attack?"

She scrambled to her feet, stubbornness radiating off her.

"I'm sure my wife, Alice, called," the man offered. "I'm Stan Mabry, by the way. That man drove up and had a small boy with him. He demanded food and my new maroon truck. My wife got the food, and then I sent her out of harm's way to call law enforcement. The guy didn't even seem to care that my wife left. He was more concerned with getting away. As he was tearing out of the drive, this young lady pulled up."

"Do you need medical care?" he asked Bristol.

"No, I'm fine. But I think the guy knew it was me. Instead of trying to avoid me, he aimed the truck right at my car."

"You sure you're all right?"

"Yes. Can we get on the road? Please."

"I'll call this in on the way." Chandler quickly got the make and model of the man's truck.

A white SUV pulled down the drive, a deputy's car following close behind. An older woman with curly black hair got out of the SUV, hurried to Stan and gave him a hug.

It took a minute to brief Deputy Joyner. Bristol remained quiet except to answer a few questions. When they were done, he turned to her. "Would you like to ride along with me?"

"I suppose I have little choice."

The deputy looked up. "I can give her a ride."

She glanced at Chandler. "I can ride with Chandler."

He probably shouldn't have agreed, but he was relieved she wanted to go with him. This was one case Chandler didn't want to go awry.

You don't take your job seriously enough, son. If you don't settle down and pay attention to what you're doing, someone's going to pay for your carelessness. Chandler reached into his pocket, pulled his dad's lighter out and flicked it open and shut several times. The lighter had been a present for his dad from him and Sydney for Christmas. His dad's words had irritated him that day years ago, but he had simply written off his dad's criticism as him being a worrier.

His dad wouldn't have to be concerned about his slackness ever again.

Chandler returned the lighter to his pocket. After he and Bristol were in his truck and had turned out of the driveway, he looked at her. "Let me call this in."

He relayed the information to Hattie. His gaze went to Bristol as he talked. "The suspect still has the boy with him."

After he disconnected, he turned to her. "I'm sorry."

"No need. You didn't do anything."

He wished he could take away her worry, but it would be useless to try. Probably even annoy her. "Was Spencer okay? Like, was he injured?"

Emotion reflected in her eyes, and she turned away and glanced at the ceiling of his truck. "I heard him calling for me."

Chandler noted her hands shook. She was doing everything in her power not to break down. "I realize you're scared, but we need to figure out where Rex will go next. I want to find him just as bad as you."

"I doubt that."

He nodded and drew a deep breath. "You're right. But I want to find your boy. Where would Rex go?"

"I don't know. He used to drive trucks in this area, plus who knows where all he went when he was buying and selling drugs. I suppose he made contacts all over the place."

Chandler didn't want to bring it up, but he felt they needed to get this out of the way. "Why did the guy say you helped sell drugs?"

"You've got to be kidding me. Right?" She glared and then glanced out the passenger window. "Because I was the mastermind of the Edwards family's drugs," she whispered like they were in a conspiracy, sarcasm blaring strong. "I have a son and am becoming a schoolteacher, so I can make lots of contacts."

He cleared his throat. Her face burned red as she glared at him. Because he'd insulted her with the question? Or something else? "Maybe I should've asked why you think the masked man would say that?"

She turned back to him, and her face scrunched into a scowl. "To throw you off. Rex is manipulative. Not only did he want to get away, but he wanted to cast doubt on me, too. Perfect revenge for a wife who had the audacity to turn him in to the authorities and then leave him. And, yes, I turned him in."

Since Chandler already knew that, he didn't say anything more to her answer. "Do you know Mia?"

"Mia was his first wife. She disappeared months before he started dating me."

"Which meant he'd used the name Mia as a threat."

Chandler had thought the same thing about the man wanting to cast doubt on Bristol. And even though he'd read in the case profile that Rex had been married previously, he was certain the document hadn't mentioned foul play but claimed the wife had left Rex. Chandler aimed his truck toward the highway. "Besides Rex, is there anyone else who would want to harm you?"

"No one. I stay to myself and live a quiet life." Defensiveness radiated off her. "After my mom died, I had no family left. I married Rex, and it's obvious what a disaster that turned out to be. I work the day shift at the diner while Spencer is at daycare, and I attend online college classes at night after I put him to bed. For the last four years, my life has been relatively boring, which is how I prefer it."

"I understand."

"I doubt that."

Chandler understood the desire for normalcy more than she realized, but he didn't take the bait. She was understandably upset and would probably welcome someone to take her anger out on. "You know, this guy may not be Rex."

She cleared her throat and turned toward the window.

His cell phone rang. "Hey, Josie. Did you learn something?"

"I sure did. You're barking up the wrong tree."

Even though the call wasn't on speakerphone, it was quiet enough in the cab for Bristol to hear. "What makes you say that?"

"Rex Edwards never made it to Huntsville. He was stabbed to death last week. Warden believes another inmate is to blame. His body was removed from the prison morgue and turned over to the local funeral home. He was cremated this morning."

He and Bristol exchanged glances. "Well, that changes our direction. Thanks for letting me know, Josie." After he disconnected, he turned to Bristol. "Did you hear that?"

"I did, but I can't believe it. If Rex is dead, then who has my son?"

The thought of Bristol's boy being in the possession of a drug dealer—and probably a killer—made Chandler's stomach twist into knots. But at least they would've had leads as to where Rex would take Spencer. Now they had nothing.

"I don't know who has your son or why. But I'm going to do everything in my power to bring him home. Maybe the masked man was Rex's friend or an accomplice. And that means you shouldn't be in direct danger."

"That's a slight relief."

The passenger-side window exploded, glass showering the cab, and a bullet lodged in the dash.

Bristol screamed.

"Get down! Get down!" Chandler hit the gas as more gunshots peppered the back window.

Adrenaline raced through his veins as he fought to keep his truck on the road while dodging bullets. The realization hit him—not only was this no random kidnapping, but someone wanted Bristol to pay. With her life.

FOUR

Bristol's knees dug into the floorboard as she leaned across the passenger seat, her hands covering her head. Glass continued to rain down on her. She tried to make herself as small as possible. Chandler bent across the seat, barely glancing over the dash as he hit the brakes and slid through what must be a curve.

"Where are the shots coming from?" she shouted. "Was he beside the road or in the truck?"

Chandler glanced in his rearview mirror and removed a gun from his holster.

"No. You can't shoot. Spencer is with him." The thought of her son being shot, or the driver losing control and crashing, scared her to death.

He flashed her a quick look. "I don't see the boy."

"He's in that truck. I heard him yelling. Please don't take the chance."

The deputy eased off the accelerator. "The shooter was in the maroon truck, but I don't see him behind us now. I need to call this in."

As Bristol listened to Chandler tell the dispatcher their location and repeat the description of the vehicle, her mind struggled with Rex being dead. If so, who had taken Spencer, and why? What did anyone have to gain? Surely if someone wanted to traffic children, they would've taken all six from the daycare van.

So many questions and no answers.

On a long straightaway, Chandler pulled off to the side of the highway, turned his truck around and eased back down the road at a snail's pace. His gaze appeared to survey the ditches and pastures.

"What are you doing?"

"Waiting for backup. Lover's Leap Lane is only eight miles long, with three intersecting roads. We have deputies headed this way who will close in on the location. We hope to trap the suspect and have a peaceful resolution."

She didn't miss the doubt in his tone, and she squinted at him. "You don't believe it'll work."

"Deputy Perkins is only a minute away, and Deputy Green is en route, five-minute ETA. If Green can cut the suspect off before he crosses Willow Road, I believe it'll work."

Bristol kept her eyes on her side of the road, searching for any signs the truck might be waiting for them. But as time crawled by, anxiousness built until it was about to bubble over. Finally, a female voice came over the radio.

"I'm in position."

Chandler said, "Let's move in."

Bristol's heart drummed out of control in her chest. *Please, keep Spencer safe. So much could go wrong.* She repeated the prayer over and over as they made their way down the rural highway. Another vehicle approached them, and her breath hitched. As it drew closer, she realized it was a deputy's vehicle. And then another deputy up behind them.

"No… That's Perkins and Green."

Her shoulders sagged. "We missed the truck?"

"Looks like it. I'll be right back." Chandler got out of his vehicle and visited with the other two deputies. She couldn't help but notice Deputy Hattie Perkins glanced her way several times. A few minutes later, Chandler climbed back in.

"What's the plan?"

"We're going to check out the area one more time in search of the suspect's vehicle."

Frustration settled heavily on her shoulders. The shooter had disappeared with Spencer. It was no use looking again on the road, for surely he was long gone with her son. Fifteen minutes of hunting, and Chandler talked again with the other deputies. The conclusion was to widen their search perimeter. A couple more deputies joined in.

They had to find her son, and soon. She'd always heard that the chances of survival for a kidnapping victim diminished as time went by. "Can the sheriff's department use a helicopter?"

"Sheriff Carroll is working on that right now."

"Working on it? How long can it take to get one?"

"Depends. More than likely another hour for the copter. It'd be easier if the suspect was on foot to keep his location contained, but we'll get him."

Hope dwindled as they went down road after road and through multiple small communities with no sightings of Stan Mabry's truck. Her mind raced as she tried to think where the man might have taken her son. Or was he holed up someplace close by, in a good hiding place?

Tucker whimpered in the back seat, and Bristol petted his head. "I wish the guy was still on foot. Your bloodhound would find him for us."

"You're right." Chandler glanced at his canine partner. "Tucker's the best."

Wrinkles and long ears called to her, calming her nerves a tad. No doubt allowing the bloodhound to work would be better than driving around aimlessly.

An hour later, Chandler turned to her. "I'm sorry. We've lost him again, but we'll keep looking. The helicopter is in the air."

"Can you drop me off at a car rental place?"

A stony expression fell over him. "Are you certain?"

"Yes." She wasn't trained in law enforcement, but she'd seen enough crime shows to know every minute that passed lowered the hope of finding her son. Even with her ex-husband dead, he had to be behind the kidnapping. Her mind kept returning to the prison. Someone there must know whom he had talked to.

Tension ate at Bristol as she sped down the highway. She checked her rearview mirror again. There was no other vehicle in sight except for a pickup pulling a flatbed trailer loaded with metal pipe and, thank goodness, no highway patrol. She'd been on the road for two hours, but with her son missing, it felt much longer. He could be out of the state by now. Three thirty in the afternoon and traffic barely existed. While Rex was in prison, she'd done her research on the facility, and before that, she'd paid attention to other drug dealers in the area. After finding the drugs in her coat, she had become almost obsessed with trying to figure out who was a part of Rex's criminal life. Who was just a friend, and who was up to no good? Almost like a stalker or private detective, she'd even followed some of his closest friends.

Thanks to Bristol, Barry Blackburn and Victor Cannon had been arrested at the same time as Rex. Barry was in his thirties and had been released three years ago. According to what Bristol learned, he came from money, and his family had paid big bucks to a Houston lawyer who'd helped him get only a year behind bars. It didn't hurt that Barry had graduated with a degree in finance and worked at an investment firm—all the things that looked solid on paper. Even people who came from good families could get involved with drugs.

Victor Cannon, in his fifties, was still serving his sentence. He had three ex-wives and had done time in Shreveport for various crimes before moving to North Texas, where he'd met Rex. He would be worth visiting to learn about Rex's most recent activities.

As she passed a compact car that had suitcases tied to the top and a laundry basket plastered against the back window, she thought about Rex's other friends. Rufus, Steve and Charlie. Which ones were just coworkers and which ones participated in the drug dealing? Her mind swirled in so many directions, she fought to bring the thoughts into focus. Her son's life hung in the balance, so she couldn't afford to get flustered. There had been nothing in the prison files to indicate the names of the guards or which building Rex had been housed in. Bristol read blogs on the prisons, many comments left by family members of inmates or ex-prisoners themselves. Occasionally, a spouse or parent would complain about inhumane treatment or poor medical care. Last summer, a facility had three inmates die due to no air-conditioning in the Texas heat, according to the article. Rex had not been at the facility.

She pulled off the highway after the next town and turned down a county road. A mile or so later, a large sign announced the prison. A generous watermelon field lay on her left and a few people in orange jumpsuits pulled weeds while a guard on horseback looked on.

Unless the sheriff's deputies found the suspect quickly, it was important she learn who'd had something to gain. Her focus returned to the task before her. She just needed to know whom Rex had been talking to. A guard or an inmate? Who had told Rex about Spencer?

Anything to learn who had her son.

After Chandler dropped Bristol off at the car rental place, he called the department to see how the helicopter search was going. He realized the importance of finding an abducted child quickly and was frustrated they hadn't located the Delaney boy yet. Bristol had been lucky to spot the suspect and the boy at that farm, but he'd gotten away again. She'd been so close.

"Any word on the chopper yet?"

Deputy Joyner was manning the desk. "Brice is supposed to be getting in the air as we speak, and four deputies are on the ground."

"Thanks. Let me know if they learn anything."

"Will do."

Chandler understood Bristol's anxiousness to find her son. Instead of going back to the station, he drove by a couple of places Rex used to hang out. Not that he thought the kidnapper was Rex, but maybe a buddy who hung out at the same places. After Chandler's dad disappeared, he had made numerous visits to several hangouts. They weren't the kind of joints he could take Bristol to.

He drove to a known drug house out on Little River Drive. Even though it was in the boonies, this place had to sit on the most-traveled red dirt road that ever existed. He parked down the road about forty yards from the house. Within fifteen minutes, he'd counted twenty-two cars coming and going. Without a search warrant, he couldn't go in, but he listened. There was no sign of Spencer Delaney or the maroon truck the suspect had gotten away in.

Suddenly, a knock sounded on his driver's-side window. Chandler glanced up.

A brawny guy covered in tattoos with a missing front tooth stood there. "Can I help you?"

No doubt this guy noticed Chandler's K-9 unit uniform and knew he was with the sheriff's department. He probably had more powerful guns than him and the guy definitely had numerous friends to help him should a fight break out. "You can. You don't happen to have any children in that house, do you?"

The man frowned. "No, we don't. Is this about that kidnapping?"

"Yes, it is." It surprised Chandler the man knew about it, but then again, maybe not. A lot of these people listened to police scanners.

The ridiculously muscular man held up his hands. "I may not be the cream of society, but I don't take kids. And I wouldn't harbor one, either. If I hear anything, Deputy…"

"Deputy Murphy."

"If I hear anything, Deputy Murphy, I'll call."

"I'd appreciate it." As Chandler pulled away, he glanced in his mirror and noticed the man had already disappeared. The funny thing was that Chandler believed him when he'd said he wouldn't harbor a kid. Most people, even criminals, had their moral lines.

He called Josie to see if she had learned anything about Rex's connections since he went to prison.

"Hey, Chandler. I'm still working on it. I've requested his phone records and am waiting to hear back."

He pulled onto a paved road. "I'm certain the sheriff's department has also asked for the call history."

"I thought of someone who might get you information faster."

"Who's that?" He'd do almost anything to have a solid lead and not be searching blindly.

"Anthony Hatfield. He was in the Roach Unit with Rex."

"Hatfield. That's right. He'd be a good one to question. Thanks, Josie." But instead of calling, he would pay the prisoner a visit. Sometimes you could get more out of an inmate when they weren't worried about their calls being recorded. It frequently didn't go well for those who gave information, and their talk was less likely to be recorded in the visitation room than over the phone.

As he merged onto the main highway, his thoughts went back to Bristol. What was she doing? He hoped she wasn't doing anything like visiting farms again. Hopefully, she'd learned her lesson.

FIVE

Even though she'd never visited a prison, she'd read enough articles put out for families to learn what to expect, so when a guard walked out to her car, she wasn't surprised. She rolled down her window.

"Who are you here to see?"

"Victor Cannon."

The younger man had a clipboard and flipped through several sheets. "Okay. Raise your hood."

She held her breath and did as he asked. He looked under the hood and glanced in the back seat.

"You can go in."

"Thank you and have a good day." She shot him a smile and pulled into the designated parking lot for visitors.

Once inside the first block building, she signed in and went through the security check, much like at the airport. The man behind a desk called on his phone, "Cannon, Victor."

A bulky security gate clicked, indicating it had unlocked. A glance up showed a guard in a tower watching her. Her heart picked up the pace. Visiting the prison was much more intimidating than what she'd expected. This was a side of life she didn't want to see, but here she was, Bristol Delaney, soon-to-be-schoolteacher, going inside a prison.

A female guard stood behind a counter as she walked through the front door. "You're here to see Victor Cannon?"

"Yes, ma'am." She again smiled. *Stop acting nervous, Bristol. The lady is watching you.*

"Don't believe Victor has ever had any visitors."

"Hmm." She could feel the guard's gaze on her, but Bristol leaned against the counter and stared at the white wall.

"You can wait in there until you're called."

She nodded and walked into a waiting room. Several minutes later, her name was announced on a speaker. She was directed into a long room that felt more like a hallway, except glass separated her from an adjoining room.

The guard pointed. "Third seat down."

Tennis balls cut in half cushioned the feet of a scuffed brown plastic chair. She glanced at the other visitors but didn't make eye contact with any of the prisoners. Several slow minutes passed before a door opened at the other end of the room and a guy dressed in an orange jumpsuit strode in. He seemed to have significantly aged since he was sentenced four years ago.

Long, curly gray hair rested on his shoulders and a variety of barbed-wire tattoos covered his biceps, neck and hands. Dark, questioning eyes took her in. She stared back, trying to appear confident under his scrutiny but afraid he saw right through her nervousness.

"Who are you?" He sat in the chair opposite her.

"You were one of Rex Edwards's friends. I wanted to find out more about his death and thought you could help me."

Victor busted out laughing and clapped his hands. "Friends with Rex? He wasn't a friend to anyone. Now—" his gaze looked her up and down as much as the glass would allow "—what is it you really want to know?"

Her heart picked up the pace, and she swallowed the lump in her throat. "Who did he share a cell with? Who did he talk to?"

A smirk crossed his lips. "This ain't federal prison, lady, like they show in the movies. This is the state. There are fifty inmates per cell."

She tried not to react. Fifty inmates? Then her ex-husband could've talked to many people. His trail might be impossible to follow. She needed more information.

"Why did you come to me, sweetheart?" He licked his lips and stared at her, the sly grin remaining in place.

He was trying to intimidate her. But with him in prison, she didn't want to let him know that when she had turned Rex in, that information had also connected her ex to Victor, thus leading to his arrest. Did he realize that?

"You trying to figure out who killed Rexy boy?"

She nodded. "That would help."

"I don't know." He shook his head, the gleam never leaving his eyes. The man glanced over his shoulder at another inmate and then to the guard who stood in the doorway. "I'd like to know who did Rex in so I could shake his hand."

Bristol resisted the urge to turn and look at the men he seemed to be communicating with.

A voice came over an intercom. "McCullough, Humphrey and Long, your visitation is over."

The younger woman beside Bristol got to her feet. "This is not right," she said to the older man on the other side of the glass—probably her father. "I drove over three hours for this visit, and they should let family know if they're going to cut it short. I can't come back for another three weeks."

"Love you, baby," the man replied.

Why hadn't they said Victor Cannon's name?

It took thirty seconds or so for the other visitors to file out of the room.

The younger lady questioned the guard as she pointed at Bristol. "Why does she get to stay?"

"You can see your daddy next time, Veronica."

The lady mumbled something Bristol couldn't understand as she exited the room, leaving her alone with the guard. She turned to the older man, his thin gray hair combed to the side but failing to cover the bald spot on his head.

She climbed to her feet, but as she tried to go past, the guard's hand clamped down on her shoulder. "Hold on, Miss Delaney."

His eyes were dull. Unlike the gleam in Victor's eyes, his gaze was dead.

"I'd like to leave now." A bad feeling gripped her stomach. She glanced at the camera positioned in the corner of the room. The guard would know he was being filmed and wouldn't do anything stupid. Right? Was the sound being recorded? Or maybe the cameras weren't working.

"You were asking questions about Rex Edwards. I'll need you to come with me."

She didn't budge. Something about this seemed off. *Be firm, not a coward.* People liked to take advantage of cowards. "No. I'm ending my visit."

He looked at her then, really looked, and slowly his jaw tensed. "You don't have a choice. The investigation is ongoing. You give me trouble, and you'll pay a hefty price."

Before she could respond, he gripped her bicep and tugged her from the room. A glance back, and she saw Victor still sitting, a victorious smile tugging at his mouth.

As the guard led her down one hall and then another, she tried to keep her voice from trembling. "Where are you taking me?"

"Quit asking questions. You'll learn soon enough."

They passed a couple of restrooms, and then he shoved her toward a cramped room where the door stood open. The sign outside read Authorized Personnel Only.

"Right here."

Two vending machines, a narrow table and two chairs filled the space. A coffeepot sat on a short counter. No doubt this was some kind of break room, but nothing about this felt like an official interview. The name of the warden had been listed on the outside of the building, but she had paid no attention. "I demand to see the warden."

The guard shrugged. "Demand all you want." He smiled and left the room.

She pulled on the door, and it opened. Relief he hadn't locked it surprised her, and she decided to leave before the guard returned. She could try to find information from the county coroner. Probably would've been a smarter idea to go there first, anyway. As she stepped into the hallway, two men were striding her way. One was in an orange jumpsuit, and the other was another guard.

The guard said, "Please step back inside the room, Miss Delaney."

"I'd like to leave."

The man dressed in the orange jumpsuit grabbed her. "Get yourself back into the room like Henry said."

"Take it easy, Gary. We just need to question her." The guard turned to her. "I'm Henry Wynne, ma'am. Could you please step back inside? I'd rather no one else hear our conversation."

Henry's eyes were kind and his mannerisms calm. Maybe she could learn information that could lead her to the kidnapper. Still…

As if he read her indecision, he said, "This won't take long and then you'll be free to go."

"Okay, but leave the door open." As she stepped inside, she prayed she'd made the right decision. "All this is because I asked about Rex?"

"I'm afraid so." Henry smiled. Gary, the gruff prisoner, remained outside, for which she was glad. "Would you care for a bottle of water or something to snack on?"

"No, thanks." Her mind swirled, trying to figure out what all this was about.

"Bristol Delaney, you're Rex Edwards's ex-wife. Word has gotten around it was your statements that put him and a few others behind bars."

Her chest grew tight, and she forced herself not to respond. But she couldn't stop her knees from shaking. How did they know she'd turned Rex in?

Henry put a dollar in a machine and pushed a button. A package of cheese crackers fell. "I suppose you heard Rex was killed a couple of days ago, and that's why you're here."

"Yes." She debated whether she should ask Henry about whom Rex had talked to and spent time with. It threw her that someone had had her removed from the visitation room. Since she had traveled some distance to ask questions, she drew a deep breath and tried to keep her voice down so only he could hear. "Can you help me? I'd like to know who Rex spent time with."

His eyebrows arched before a smile crossed his lips. "He was in a cell with fifty other inmates. Prisoners come and go. It'd be difficult to nail down all the names without knowing exactly what you're looking for."

It was time to come clean. "My son was taken this morning—kidnapped. At first, I believed it was Rex, because I can't think of another reason someone would want a three-year-old boy unless he was the father. After I learned someone had killed Rex, I figured he must've still been involved in organizing the kidnapping but had been killed before he could carry out his scheme. I need to learn who that person or persons are."

Henry shook his head. "To my understanding, you kept the boy from him. That's a cruel blow, especially to a man like Rex."

Tension built in the room. How did he know about Spencer? "I had my reasons. I'm not trying to cause problems. I just want my son back and have no idea where else to find the person behind his abduction."

Henry opened the bag of crackers and popped one into his mouth. When he held one out to her, she shook her head.

Without warning, his hand shot out and grabbed her by the shoulder, spinning her around. His gaze penetrated hers, his eyes wild as his face moved closer to hers. "You need to back off, lady. Let the boy go."

Her heart stampeded in her chest, but she refused to give in. Spencer was all she had left. "Who has my son? I'll never stop searching until I find him."

"Then you just signed your death warrant, along with the boy's."

The guard's words sank in. This was her choice?

Quit investigating and let her son go, or keep digging and cause both their deaths?

Doom settled heavily on her shoulders. But she had been in a low place before and turned to the only being that had never let her down. *Please, God, help me.*

Suddenly anger replaced her fear. "Why? With Rex dead, why is someone determined to have Spencer? He's innocent. I'm just trying to bring my little boy home."

Henry's grip on her shirt tightened, and he tugged her closer. He ground out between his teeth, "Back off, Delaney."

Someone had bribed Henry. Or maybe they'd threatened him with something else. But he was in this just as deep as Rex had been.

"I'll keep digging. I must get my son back."

Suddenly Gary stepped into the room, grabbed her and threw her into the block wall. Her head slammed into the brick. Lights flashed before her eyes, and she fell to the ground.

"Don't kill her, Gary. Are you stupid?"

The prisoner spun. "There's no cameras back here. What are they gonna do? Throw me in jail?"

She crawled along the floor to the doorway. Anything to escape, but before she could, a large boot kicked her in the ribs. The air was knocked from her. She curled into a fetal position, gasping. Rex had hit her before, but there had only been one man. There was no reasoning with the prisoner or guard, just like it had been with her husband, so she didn't try.

"Get back in the hallway." The guard tried to shove the man out the door, but they continued to yell at one another.

She searched for a way out. No doubt they had known there would be no other guards around. The door started to close, but she got her arm into the gap and shoved it open. In a staggering effort, she climbed to her feet.

She ran down the hall and went to turn the corner. She face-planted straight into Chandler Murphy's chest.

His hands went to her arms. "Are you okay?"

Out of breath, she panted. "There—" She pointed. "A guard and another prisoner ganged up on me, trying to intimidate me."

He moved beside her and wrapped his arm around her shoulders. She leaned into his touch, thinking she'd never been so happy to see the deputy as she was right now.

SIX

Chandler's blood boiled as two men came out of what appeared to be an employee break room.

The guard's gaze took him in and then went to his uniform. "Glad to see you here, Deputy. I have everything under control now."

The prisoner glared at the guard. They weren't fooling Chandler. He could sense the tension, and by Bristol's pale complexion and panicked expression, he figured he'd just interrupted an attack. He wished Bristol hadn't jumped the gun and come to the prison without him. Since he was here... "We're working on a kidnapping case, of Rex Edwards's son. Do either of you know who Rex would've been talking to that might have committed the crime?"

"Not me. We have over twelve hundred inmates, and I can't keep up with them all."

Chandler doubted the guard didn't know what went on, but he turned to the prisoner. "What about you?"

He shrugged. "I know nothing." But his gaze landed on Bristol as if sending her a warning.

"Okay. Thanks for your time." Chandler turned to Bristol. "We have other people to interview."

She stayed beside him as they walked out into the

main lobby. When the door shut, she said, "Boy, am I glad to see you."

He forced a smile. "We'll talk in a bit. For now, come with me, but let me do the talking."

She rolled her eyes in response but said nothing. Before he came in, he had asked to see Anthony Hatfield, one of the trustees of the prison, a man who'd been here for three years. The business executive came from Jarvis County and had gotten caught embezzling money from the investment company he'd worked for. It came out at the trial that Anthony had made some poor investments and had panicked with foreclosure and bankruptcy looking him in the face.

They entered a large visitation room. Anthony sat at a small table in the corner, and a smile broke out on his face when they entered the room.

He stood and shook Chandler's hand. "Hello, Deputy Murphy. It surprised me when I heard you were here for a visit. Who's this lovely lady with you?"

The man's mannerisms seemed out of place for the setting, but Chandler supposed anyone could mess up their life. "This is Bristol Delaney, a soon-to-be teacher in Jarvis County. Her son has been kidnapped, and I'd hoped you could assist us."

"What can I do?" He glanced at Bristol before looking back to Chandler. "I've been stuck in here for three years."

"Rex Edwards was the boy's father. Thought maybe you knew him and could tell us who his friends were."

The man let out a soft whistle. "I knew Edwards. Not that I spent time with him or talked to him. He was a man best to avoid. I suppose you're aware he died several days ago, right before he was set to be released."

"That's what we understand. Bristol believes who-ever took her son was connected to Rex."

Hatfield's eyebrows furrowed. "I'm sorry to hear that. Rex was a quiet but dangerous man. Others sur-rounded him, but there were two men who never left his side—a guard by the name of Henry Wynne, and Victor Cannon."

He and Bristol exchanged glances. Chandler asked, "He was close to a guard?"

"Yeah, but that's not unusual, even though it's not supposed to happen."

He would have Josie check out Henry Wynne's con-nections as soon as he was back in his truck. "Is there someone who was recently released that he hung out with?"

"People come and go." Anthony glanced up at the ceiling tiles. "Let me think. No. Wait. There was one man. McGinnis. Didn't know his first name. I think he got transferred to Huntsville for release."

He'd have to remember that name. "What about phone calls or contacts from the outside?"

"I wouldn't know much about that." Anthony glanced over his shoulder before turning back to Chandler. His hands fidgeted on the table, and he lowered his voice. "It seemed Rex received a lot of calls and made a few recently. And someone must've been keeping him in spending money, because he seemed to have plenty of it."

"Do you know who?" From the corner of his eye, Chandler caught Bristol leaning forward.

"No." Again, he looked around the room. He hesi-tated and scratched his neck like he had something to say but was uncertain.

"What is it?" Chandler prodded.

"I don't know if it's true, but I heard through the grapevine Sheriff Carroll called earlier today to ask questions. He wanted to know who Rex had been talking to."

Disappointment hovered that the information wasn't more helpful. "That's not surprising the sheriff would inquire, considering Rex's son was abducted. Just part of the investigation."

The ex-businessman shook his head. "I don't know if this is true, but word has it he was asking questions—" his voice dropped even lower, making him difficult to hear "—about Simon Murphy. If Rex ever told anyone where the body was buried."

"My dad?"

Anthony nodded.

That could mean the sheriff wanted to know if Rex had told his secret. Or *their* secret, as in Rex's and the sheriff's. Or maybe the sheriff was still looking into Chandler's dad's case. He swallowed to clear his throat. "Okay. Thanks."

"I hope you find your son soon, ma'am."

Bristol gave him a slight smile, but her blue eyes searched his. Had she been able to hear Anthony's whispers?

Chandler thanked the man for his time, and he and Bristol walked out into the parking lot together.

As they neared her car, he turned to her. "That was dangerous, coming here by yourself."

She glared. "This is a prison, with guards and cameras. It should've been safe."

He released a deep breath. "Yeah, it should've been, but, Bristol, someone killed Rex here just a few days ago. Sheriff Carroll talked with the warden earlier, and they believe his killer was an inmate. Who were you here to see?"

Her lips pressed together. "Same as you. I came to visit with an inmate."

"Who?" he repeated.

"Victor Cannon. He was arrested shortly after Rex."

Chandler remembered Cannon. He'd dealt drugs with Rex. "Did you learn anything more than what Anthony told us?"

Her shoulders dropped. "No. A minute after I sat down, the other visits were cut short, and the inmates and visitors cleared from the room. That's when Henry Wynne came in and forced me to the break room."

"You took a chance coming here." He tried to keep his tone neutral, but how could he expect to keep her safe if she didn't keep him in the loop? "They haven't figured out who Rex's killer was yet. You want to ride with me in my truck?"

"No. I don't need protecting." She held up her hand. "Wait. I take that back. I'm glad you showed up when you did, but I'm used to doing things on my own."

He stared at her. The defensiveness. The stubbornness. "I get the desire to be independent, but please quit going off on your own until we have your son back and whoever is behind the attacks is behind bars."

She let out a sigh. "I understand."

Hypocrite. The word came to his mind as he opened her car door for her. Ever since his father disappeared, Chandler had retreated into his own world. He hadn't been a good team player, preferring to investigate cases alone.

She soothed her jeans like she was restless. "Are you headed back to Liberty?"

Even though he'd rather work alone, he didn't want

Bristol driving back by herself or deciding to interview anyone else without him. "I'm headed to the coroner's office. Do you want to go with me?"

Her head popped up. "Yeah, I do. How about I follow you?"

"Works for me." He pulled out of the prison a few minutes later with Bristol's rental car in his rearview mirror. Maybe instead of fighting her tagging along, he needed to get used to the idea. A churning in his gut surprised him. He'd dated little in the last five years. But that had been the plan until his dad's case was solved. The need to remain focused drove him to not be distracted. The thought of spending time with Bristol didn't bother him, which was surprising since he'd had little interest in seeing anyone. Maybe it was because he felt like she could relate.

Her car pulled up beside his in the parking lot. She walked so fast to the door that he chalked it up to being eager like him. At the front desk, he asked for Dr. Dunlap. The young guy behind the desk glanced from him to Bristol. "Your name?"

"Deputy Murphy from Jarvis County."

"Hold on." The guy used the phone and then nodded toward the hall. "Second door past the water fountain."

"Thanks." They walked to the end of the dimly lit passageway.

A gray-haired man with glasses perched on the end of his nose looked up. "What can I help you with, Deputy Murphy?"

"I came to ask you about Rex Edwards, a man you examined the other night."

"From the prison."

"Yes," Chandler replied.

"Some of the information is privileged. What would you like to know?"

Bristol stepped up. "Can you tell us about his death? Do they know who committed the murder?"

The coroner frowned. "It's not my job to determine who killed the man. Just the cause of death."

Chandler realized Bristol was impatient to learn details, and he hoped the coroner wouldn't be put off. "Have you learned the cause of death yet?"

"Sure. It wasn't difficult. An eight-inch stab wound through the back to the left bronchus of the lung."

That was no surprise. "Anything unusual?"

"The victim had nineteen lacerations to the face and neck area."

But Rex was stabbed in the back. "Were there defensive wounds?"

"No."

"Then why was his face cut up?" Bristol turned to Chandler.

"I don't know. Rage, maybe. The killer probably hated the victim, or he wouldn't have stabbed him."

He noted Bristol's face had turned crimson, a sure indication she found the doctor's answers annoying.

She continued with the questions. "Is it common to receive bodies from the prison?"

"Occasionally." He shrugged. "No one's too upset, and it saves the taxpayers' money."

Chandler schooled his reaction. "True. Of course, I suppose it's up to the courts to give the criminals the death penalty."

The man chuckled. "I get your point, but many consider it doing the world a favor. Is there anything else?"

"Yes, I have one," Bristol interjected. "Is it normal to have the bodies cremated so soon?"

"If no family comes to claim the body, certainly." Dr. Dunlap glanced at the clock on the wall.

"Thank you." Chandler looked at Bristol and took in her stiff posture. Now that he had time to think about it, he should've asked her to wait outside. He thanked the coroner and then jerked his head toward the door.

After they exited the room, he asked, "Are you okay?"

She shot him a look. "I'm fine."

But he could tell by her clipped answer, she wasn't fine. Bristol had made it no secret she was afraid of her ex-husband. Even so, she'd married the guy and had his child. Maybe losing the man she once loved still caused her grief. "I was careless. Rex was Spencer's daddy."

She stopped dead in her tracks and held her hand up. "I hate that someday Spencer will learn who and what his daddy was. I worry what that knowledge will do to his self-esteem, but I got over my feelings for Rex years ago. I wouldn't wish anyone to be murdered, even Rex, but I was not sorry he went to prison for his crimes."

They exited the building, and Chandler decided not to comment. No doubt she wasn't in love with her ex-husband, but he wondered if she had any feelings at all for the man. He'd seen pictures of Bristol's son, blond hair and brown eyes—a weird mixture of his mom and dad. Irritation churned in Chandler's gut—something akin to jealousy that he hadn't felt since high school when Sara Ackerman dumped him for the good-looking running back on the football team.

"Where to now?" Bristol glanced at him. All previous emotion vanished.

"Let's go back to Liberty." He'd hoped they would've learned more. Any kind of clue to discover who had taken her son and why. "You want to follow me?"

"Glad to."

He did a double take to see if she'd said it sarcastically. Her blue eyes suggested she was being sincere. Bristol was a strange mixture of *leave me alone, I can do things myself* and *it'd be nice to have someone to lean on*. Trust. Her trust had been broken by a man who had used her.

As much as he wanted to solve his dad's case—and he believed Rex was the key—Chandler didn't want to let Bristol down. He'd disappointed his parents and had no intention of doing the same thing to her.

SEVEN

Bristol followed Chandler in her rental car out of the parking lot. The image of Gary grabbing her and slamming her head into the block wall kept replaying through her mind. What if Chandler hadn't shown up? Would they have killed her and made her death look like an accident?

What would've happened to Spencer then?

The whole day had been nothing but one incident after another, and she was no closer to finding her son than when she'd first received the call from the daycare. Her head throbbed from thinking over her problems.

Don't be afraid to lean on others.

Her mama had said those words to her. Bristol had been sixteen and upset her mom had broken off a relationship with her fiancé, Kirk Canfield. Kirk was one of her mom's boyfriends who had treated Bristol like a daughter. Then her mom dumped him. Once again, she moved Bristol to a new town, leaving Kirk and her life behind. Being a frustrated teen, Bristol had shouted back at her mom that she didn't need anyone, and she couldn't wait to get out on her own. Away from *her*.

She'd aimed to prove she could make it alone.

Little did Bristol realize her mom would die two

short years later after a prolonged case of pneumonia. Frequently, her mom's words returned to her and would make Bristol more determined to stand on her own.

But within a year of her mom's death, Bristol had met and married Rex. She convinced herself she wasn't leaning on him, that their relationship was mutual. He was her choice. Even when he started forbidding her to do things or go places, she told herself everything was fine. She was happy. Deep down, she realized she was in denial. Fear that she had turned out just like her mom kept her going. Anything but admit she'd made a mistake. If she tried to make their marriage work, it would succeed.

She followed Chandler down the highway, and when they stopped at Grub, Gas, and Go for fuel and something to eat, she wondered if she should continue on without him. The deputy bought water for Tucker and fed him from the stash of food in the back of his truck. She watched the man interact with his dog and was impressed with his care for the animal. Rex had yelled at the neighborhood animals, threatening to hurt them if any came near him. Thankfully, the dogs either stayed clear or barked from a distance.

Before they got back in their vehicles, she asked, "Have you heard from the sheriff? Any word about the search with the helicopter?"

He frowned. "Nothing yet."

She sighed. "Will they keep looking into the night?"

"Doubtful. But if Spencer isn't found before morning, I'm sure the department will search again. I know that's not what you wanted to hear."

No, it wasn't, but it did no good to take her frustrations out on him. "Is anyone checking into Rex's phone records or who's been putting money into his account?"

"Besides Deputy Joyner, Josie Hunt with Bring the Children Home Project is looking into the case. All of it takes time."

"I know. Be patient."

"I didn't say that. We're doing all that we can."

Defensiveness in Chandler's tone caught her attention, eliciting a double take. He lowered his chin and shoved his hands in his jeans' pockets. The deputy's five-o'clock shadow gave him a rough and attractive look. His K-9 uniform of a navy polo shirt and cap with the search-and-rescue emblem had its appeal. But it was his intense hazel eyes that drew her attention—a strange mixture of golden brown and green staring at her, seeming like he could read her thoughts. How long had it been since she'd noticed a more handsome man? Rex popped into her mind. A laugh bubbled up into her throat. The captivation with her ex had been superficial and soon turned so sour it was difficult to even look at the man. Chandler, on the other hand, had done nothing but grow more attractive with his caring demeanor. "I appreciate everything you've done for me."

Her rare compliment evoked a head nod, which was good enough for her.

A few minutes later, they were on the road and making good time. It was late in the day, and the deli sandwich she'd picked up at the convenience store had little taste. Time passed like molasses in wintertime, but she wasn't sure what to do next except continue searching for information. She knew Chandler and the authorities were doing all they could. She hoped it was sufficient.

Barely any cars were on the road when they were about forty-five minutes from Liberty. It'd be dark in a couple of hours, and then the helicopter would call it quits for the night. She must've been daydreaming, for

Chandler was getting a bit ahead of her. After the big curve ahead, she planned to pick up her speed. As she eased through the turn, something rained down on her car, hitting her hood and windshield. Shiny prisms littered the pavement.

A thunderous blast made her jump. Her right front tire blew, sending the vehicle out of control.

Brake lights came on in front of her, and Chandler's truck came flying back toward her. She fought the steering wheel for control, but the car continued toward the ditch. She jerked the wheel again, managing to keep it on the road. Her car slowed, and then *thump, thump, thump* filled the air until Chandler blocked her path.

He jumped out and ran to her door, yanking it open. "Get out. Hurry. Get in my truck."

Barely able to make sense out of what was happening, she did as he said. She ran to the passenger side of his truck and jumped in.

His foot hit the gas pedal, and they took off with the tires squealing.

"What's happening?" She glanced behind them.

"There was a guy on the side of the road hurling handfuls of nails at your car."

She glanced behind them. A maroon truck pulled out from the brush where the nails had been thrown. "He was waiting for me?"

"Looks like it. And I'm certain I saw your son standing in the passenger seat." Chandler's speed climbed higher as he took the winding road too fast.

Suddenly, gunfire exploded behind them.

"Get down."

Not again. So much for making it on her own. Once more she found herself in the protection of Chandler Murphy.

He gritted his teeth as more shots rained into the cab. "I need to get this guy off my bumper. Tucker, down."

Still on her knees, she glanced in the side mirror, hoping to catch a glimpse of her son, but they were too far away. The other truck gained speed, and Chandler held his gun in his hand. They skidded to a stop and then took off again. Where were they headed? Bristol started to peek over the seat, but he yelled, "Stay down!"

She glanced over her shoulder at him. "Where are we headed?"

"Just trying to get away at the moment." He hit his mic. "Shots fired. We're on Carter's Trail…"

Static filled the air, followed by "…again."

He hit the button and repeated his location. There was no answer. After a second, he said, "The maroon truck has backed off."

"Is it safe to get up now?"

"I think so."

His response wasn't reassuring. As soon as she returned to her seat, she looked behind them. At first, she didn't see anyone following them, but then her gaze caught a reflection. Should she use her gun? She told herself she could protect herself, but she couldn't take the chance of hitting Spencer or causing the guy to wreck. "He's still back there."

"I know. Let me try calling in again. I don't want to lose that truck now."

"Not if Spencer is in there." She wished she knew for certain he was in the truck. If not, Chandler could take this guy out. Bristol listened as Chandler repeatedly tried, unsuccessfully, to radio into the other deputies. She put her seat belt back on but continued to keep an eye behind them. "Is that him still following us?"

Chandler glanced into his mirror, serious lines crossing his forehead. "Yes."

"Why is he doing that? What does he want?" She was glad her son might be close, but she didn't understand what the abductor wanted. She'd thought his plan was to take Spencer and run.

"I don't know. Bristol, since we know this guy isn't Rex Edwards, we need to figure out who has your boy and why."

"I realize that." Irritation crawled all over her, trying to figure out what this guy wanted. At least he'd backed off. They continued down the highway, taking curves and hills much too fast. "Do you know where we're at?"

"Not really. Headed farther away from Liberty. That's for certain." He glanced in the rearview mirror again.

"Is there a way we get Spencer back without taking a chance he'll be hurt? If he's still in the vehicle with this guy, we're so close to him I can hardly stand it."

"I know. I keep thinking about that, too." He nodded at her. "Try your cell phone. See if you get a signal. If we had help, we could squeeze this guy in between our two vehicles, or we could put down spike strips."

"Wouldn't the spikes cause the driver to lose control?" And if her son wasn't in the truck, and they hurt the kidnapper, Spencer may never be found.

"Could, but we'd be better off to get Spencer back now."

"You're not going to take this guy out, are you?" Her heart pounded in her chest. Fear that Chandler would try to take the guy down at this speed scared her most of all. Her stomach swirled into knots at the thought. So much could go wrong, and everything could lead to her son being injured. She didn't know if she could take the chance. But she couldn't expect Chandler to just drive around, either. She glanced at her phone. "There are no bars. I can't believe there are still places that don't get a signal."

"Looks like our man is coming for us again."

Sure enough, the maroon truck was getting bigger in her mirror. Suddenly, an older white BMW coupe pulled out on the highway in front of them. When Chandler swung wide to pass the vehicle, the car swerved to the middle of the road, blocking his path.

He ground out, "Looks like we have more company."

The BMW slowed, and the truck grew closer. Bristol's breath hitched. "They're going to sandwich us in like we were planning to do. I don't want Spencer to get hurt."

Chandler flicked his cell at her. "Use mine again. Keep trying to call until you get someone. Scroll down in my contacts and call Sheriff Carroll or Bring the Children Home Project."

She hurried to do his bidding, but just then the truck rammed into their bumper, snapping her head against the headrest. The first name that showed on his list was Bring the Children Home Project, and she hit the number. Nothing. A glance at the screen showed no bars. "You're not getting a signal."

"Surely we'll get a signal somewhere in here."

Brake lights flashed in front of them before they slammed into the back of the coupe just as the truck hit them from behind. The jolt sent lights dancing in front of her eyes. "Get us out of here!"

"I'm trying."

"Don't hurt Spencer!" She knew the deputy realized he needed to be careful, but she couldn't help but say it again.

The car in front of them increased the distance, but Chandler held back even though the truck closed in.

Against his better judgment, their speed increased to over sixty on the country highway. The pavement offered no shoulder and wove with the winding landscape.

When Chandler slowed for a curve, the truck hit him again. Chandler's truck fishtailed, and just as a bridge approached, he got it back under control. A long straightaway appeared ahead, and their speed climbed to eighty.

"We're going too fast."

"I need to get the BMW out of the way so I can concentrate on the truck behind us. Shoot at the car."

"Okay." She dug her nine-millimeter out and took aim out her window. When they topped the hill, the coupe slowed again, and the truck sped up. She pulled the trigger just as they were rammed from behind, knocking the gun out the window. Her head slammed into the headrest as the BMW's back windshield shattered on the passenger side.

Chandler yelled, "Hang on!"

The words were no more said than she realized the bridge went over the railroad tracks. Trees lined the highway, and a long train went under the road. Chandler tried to slow, but the truck hit him from behind. He slammed on his brakes, but the truck kept pushing, the smell of rubber filling the air.

"Train!" Bristol gripped the dash, her knuckles turning white.

Their speed decreased more, but it wasn't enough. Their truck was pinned between the two vehicles and propelled toward the edge of the pavement.

"Stop, Chandler!"

"I can't. Brace for impact!"

Her fingers dug into the dash and every muscle tensed. *God, help us!*

Chandler fought for control, but his truck continued to slide toward the drop-off, the train whizzing underneath them. She leaned back in her seat, and her foot bore down on the floorboard as if it could help slow them down. The treetops blurred by his driver's window, and the roar of the train combined with the screeching brakes blared in her ears.

"Stop!" she squealed.

"Hold on." He fumbled for his Glock and hung it out of the driver's-side window toward the car in front of them. Four quick shots and the driver sped away. He hit the gas, but the truck continued shoving him toward the edge. The front driver's tire dipped over the pavement and suspended over the side.

"I'm getting out of here!" Bristol screamed.

"No!"

With her hand on the door handle, his truck balanced on the edge. She held her breath, afraid to move. Chandler threw it in Reverse and hit the gas.

But the other truck had backed up and had a running start. *Oh, no! Spencer!*

The guy slammed into their truck, and even as they were falling, she turned to see if the other vehicle fell off the bridge. But everything was a blur.

With a jolt, they landed on the moving railroad cars, suspended between two boxcars.

Chandler's shoulder burned like fire, with every nerve throbbing, making his whole body hurt. He squeezed his eyes shut, trying to clear his senses. A loud roar rang in his ears.

"Oh. My neck hurts."

He tuned to the voice but couldn't figure out who was speaking. He searched for the sound, a blurry fig-

ure moving next to him. A groan sounded, and he realized it came from within him.

"Are you hurt?"

"What?" He let out a breath and leaned against a
door. Was he in his truck?

"Chandler? Oh, no, you're bleeding!"

Couldn't be. He forced his eyes open again and stared
at the woman beside him. Bristol Delaney. What was
she doing with him? Wait. Her son was missing. *That's
it.* Slowly, everything came back to him, including the
chase.

A hand touched his back. "You're bleeding. We must
get off this train so you can get help."

"Train?" The constant rumble and movement had
him looking out the windshield. Green scenery whizzed
by, amplifying his wooziness. They were riding a train.
No, his *truck* was riding on top of a train. They were in
the middle of the Texas wilderness, and he had no idea
what the nearest town was.

"Chandler, we have to get off this train and see if
Spencer was in the other vehicle." Bristol twisted in
her seat and looked out the back window. "What if the
truck ran off the bridge?"

The boy. They had to find Bristol's boy. "I saw the
maroon truck. It didn't get off the road."

"Are you certain?" Her gaze searched his face for
confirmation.

"Yes." Wetness slid up the back of his neck. He flinched
with startling surprise when he turned. "Tucker. Are you
all right?"

The dog licked the back of his neck again.

"I'm okay, fella." He rubbed the bloodhound's fur.
As his senses returned, the pain intensified, but he had
to shove away the anguish right now. He glanced to

Bristol's huge blue eyes as her look of concern intensified. "I'm okay. You're right. We have to find a way down from here."

Blood cascaded across his arm and dripped to his pants leg. Either he was shot, or he'd hurt himself when his truck crashed onto the train and made the knife wound worse. It was difficult to determine how much damage his vehicle had suffered because of how much his truck leaned to the driver's side. At the very least, his front tire must've blown.

He finally got the sense to ask Bristol if she was injured.

"I'm fine. My neck hurts, but I don't think I've suffered damage. Probably just whiplash."

"Are you certain?"

"Yes. I was looking back at the maroon truck when we hit. That wasn't smart."

"Okay. Let's see if we can find a way down from this locomotive." He unbuckled his seat belt and ignored his bleeding arm. A glance behind him showed Tucker's wrinkled face close to his. Chandler moved to see around him. With no roads or towns in view, he had no idea which way they were headed. Rock was piled on the boxcars, telling him they must be headed to a railhead somewhere. His mind searched for places where there were concrete plants or road construction materials, but everything he was familiar with was farther south, toward Dallas, not east.

"How fast do you think we're going?" Bristol's voice cut through his thoughts.

"Hard to tell. Sixty or seventy. Too fast to jump, if that's what you're thinking."

She didn't respond, which told him that was exactly what had been going through her mind. As much as he wanted to catch the suspect, he knew they had to proceed with caution. *Your recklessness is going to get someone killed one day. Think before you act.* His dad's words played through his mind. He'd underestimated danger before and had no intentions of repeating his deadly mistake. No matter how badly Bristol wanted her child back.

"He could die."

As if she'd read his thoughts, Bristol referred to her son. If Chandler moved too quickly, one or both of them could die. Move too slowly and her boy could die. Wasn't much of a choice. Chandler squeezed her hand. "That will not happen. We're going to bring your son home."

His truck vibrated as the rock shifted, making them tilt even more. "Let me try my cell phone." He glanced around, checking the console and his pockets. "Where is my phone?"

"You gave it to me. Hold on." She reached into the floorboard and then between the seats, pulling out the phone. "Here it is."

He took it from her and noticed the screen was cracked. After he hit the button at the bottom, the light came on. It was hard to read, but he managed to call Bring the Children Home Project.

"This is Josie. About time you checked in."

"Listen, I need you to check my location and let me know where we are. Connection is sporadic, so hurry."

"Okay. Stand by."

Bristol eyed him.

"We have GPS. For safety reasons, we can all see where each other is. As long as we don't turn off our phones."

She nodded. "I hear you. Sounds like a good plan."

"You must be out of range. It's still showing you're at the crash site. Where are you?"

"On a train. Our suspect ran us off the road on an overpass and onto a passing train."

Josie let out a light whistle.

He gave her a brief description of what had happened and that he was injured. "We need to find the suspect now."

"Yes, sir. I'll relay your message to the team. Do you need me to contact Sheriff Carroll?"

The sheriff's department had worked with Bring the Children Home Project multiple times and was familiar with Josie. "Yes, please. I tried calling them earlier, but my—" His phone lost the signal.

The train went around a curve. They had to find a way down from here. Maybe he could crawl out of the truck and contact the engineer. Hopefully he or she had spotted their vehicle. "I'm going to have the engineer stop the train."

Bristol had been watching out the window and turned to him. "The truck keeps sliding. Can you get out without falling? Looks like we're on the edge."

A glance out his window showed their vehicle leaned precariously on the rim of the railroad car. "I'll get out on your side." He secured his Glock in his holster and stretched across the console, trying not to sit on her. She understood and scooted over, giving him room to cross over her.

"I'll be right back. You should be fine." He patted Tucker on the head. "See you in a bit, buddy." He pulled the handle, and the wind caught the door, yanking it open. He wedged his boot against the bottom of the seat and held the door open with his injured arm, shoving the pain aside. They were even with the treetops. One wrong step could prove fatal.

"Be careful."

Her words carried on the wind as he took a step onto the pile of rocks. His boot slid downward, underneath the truck. Quickly, he grabbed the side of the door opening and jerked his foot out of the sinking aggregate and onto the metal rail of the boxcar. A tumultuous gust blew his hair, and the rumble of the locomotive rang in his ears.

Whammmmmp! Whammmmmp!

The whistle made him jump. He turned his attention back to working his way to the front of the train. Using the hood for support, he walked the rail like a tightrope to the front of the boxcar. The front end of his truck hung over the car. Probably due to the loss of blood, he still felt woozy and inhaled a deep breath. *Please, Lord, help me make this jump.*

He leaped, using his arms to propel him forward, and made it to the next car. His feet dug in, and then he was back to moving across the rock, careful to keep low. Only five boxcars until he was to the engine. Quickly, he made his way across the open bin and jumped to the next car.

He felt like he was making good progress—until a voice lifted above the rumble. Tinted windows kept him from seeing inside the truck. After a second of no sound from Bristol, he moved again.

Just as he was about to leap to the next car, a horn sounded. His truck. He jerked around. Bristol and Tucker were outside the vehicle and hanging on. "Get back in!"

She pointed and yelled something unintelligible.

"What?"

She waved her hands wildly.

He turned around and looked in front of the train. A black tunnel loomed ahead. The engine had disappeared into the abyss. His heart pounded. There wasn't room for him. He'd be squashed.

Without thought, he leaped from the car to the wilderness below.

Pain shot up his feet and legs until his whole body was in agony.

Blackness descended on him, blocking out the forest floor and the sunlight. The chugging of the train faded until only a dull ringing remained.

What about Bristol and Tucker? He needed to save them. *You're going to get someone killed.* His father's words rose like a whisper, and then, blissfully, there was nothing.

EIGHT

She didn't have time to consider her options after watching, horrified, as Chandler jumped from the train. With Tucker's leash in her grasp, Bristol yelled, "Come on, boy."

She sprang from the train and prayed they survived as she flew through the air. *Roll. Roll.* The words echoed in her brain, but as she landed, her foot caught, sending her flailing through the brush, and she landed in a pile of deep grass on her hands and knees. Momentum carried her forward, and her face hit the ground, her chin digging into the soil.

She lay on the ground for several moments, trying to get her bearings. Like she'd taken a punch to her jaw, her face throbbed. The smell of grass assaulted her nose, and she realized it was because she'd face-planted into the pasture.

With a quick swipe of her chin, she glanced around. Sudden coldness hit at her core when her gaze landed on the tunnel. She was about twenty feet from death. They'd barely made it. Just a couple more seconds, and she and Tucker would've been crushed.

Tucker. Where was Tucker?

Whimpering caught her attention. The sweet bloodhound limped toward her. He must've jumped a second after her. Her heart hitched. "Are you all right?"

She struggled to her knees as Tucker licked her face. She laughed and wrapped her arm around his neck. "I'm okay, big boy."

She allowed him to show his affection as she looked around for Chandler. Where had he landed? She climbed to her feet. "Where's Chandler, boy? Help me find him."

The dog looked at her and cocked his head. She gathered his leash into her grip. What command had Chandler used? "Search, Tucker. Search for Chandler."

She waited to see if the dog understood.

The dog took off up the embankment of the railroad tracks, and she struggled to keep pace. Chandler had jumped before her, so they headed back the way they'd come.

One more glance at the tunnel, and she wondered why she hadn't heard the train's brakes. Was it possible the train personnel were not aware of the crash?

"Chandler!" She called his name, but there was no answer. Tucker continued to lead the way along the tracks. Every twenty or so seconds, she called Chandler's name, but still no response. When she was certain they'd gone far enough, she stopped and looked in the ditch for any sign of the deputy. Grass blew in the wind, and tree limbs wove back and forth. Maybe the train had traveled farther than she thought because it had been moving so fast.

Concern set in when they'd gone another fifty yards with no sign of Chandler. She tugged on the leash. "Stop, Tucker. We've gone too far."

The bloodhound ceased his sniffing and looked at her, his tail wagging.

Chandler wouldn't be this close to the tracks but had

leaped several feet away. Maybe Tucker couldn't get his scent up this high. "Okay, boy, I don't want to do this, but we're going to have to search down there."

The dog leaned against her leg. She rubbed a hand across his back, figuring he was waiting to be told what to do. "Search for Chandler."

She stepped off the left side of track and down the embankment into the weeds. At the bottom of the incline, a barbed-wire fence stretched across the space. Sparse woods lay on the other side. They wove along the edge, staying parallel to the tracks. She was about ready to turn around and try again when the dog seemed to pick up a scent. "Find Chandler, Tucker."

The bloodhound grew more excited and headed into the brush. He let out a yelp.

A boot stuck out from the scrubby plant. "Chandler!"

She hurried over and found him lying facedown on the earth. Blood soaked his arm, and dirt smeared his clothes. A couple of rips split his shirt.

"Chandler." She placed the back of her hand against his cheek. "Are you okay? Talk to me."

The deputy stirred before opening his eyes.

"It's me. Bristol. Please, talk to me. Are you okay?"

Tucker licked his partner on the cheek and then sat. "Good boy, Tucker." She wished she knew the words to let him know he'd done well. She patted his head once more.

As the dog whimpered and again licked his handler, trying to gain his attention, Chandler mumbled, "I'm okay, Tuck." But the dog continued until Chandler finally chuckled. "Okay, boy, I'm up."

Relief filled Bristol, until she noticed the deputy struggling to sit. "You're hurt."

He ignored her comment and looked around.

Confusion etched his forehead, and she guessed he was trying to figure out where they were. "You jumped from the train. You were trying to get to the engineer so we could contact the sheriff's department."

He blinked, and then realization must've dawned. "There was a tunnel."

"Yes." Well, at least it was coming back to him. She didn't want to hurry him, but Spencer was getting farther away. "Are you able to walk?"

"Of course." He climbed to his feet, and Tucker moved closer.

She noticed Chandler braced himself on the trunk of a tree.

"Let's see." He glanced back at the tracks and then to the left, where the sun dipped in the sky. "That way is west."

"Yeah, I would say so."

He patted his own pockets. "Do you have your cell phone?"

"No. I dropped it when we jumped from the train."

His eyes squinted. "I'm sorry. I wasn't thinking. Are you okay?"

"I'm fine. Sore, but no injuries."

"And…" His gaze went to Tucker, and he dropped to his knee. "You know better than to jump from a train."

The dog tilted his head sideways.

Bristol could tell that, behind his humor, genuine concern laced his voice. "Tucker seems fine now, but he had a slight limp right after we landed."

Chandler lifted the dog's right front paw. "It's a tad swollen."

At the action, Tucker licked his paw while Chandler examined him. The deputy stood. Again, he patted his pockets. He came away with his pistol and examined it, releasing the magazine. He rubbed the dirt from it and then reinserted it into the gun. "Looks okay. We need to get moving."

Even though she was thinking the same thing, she didn't comment. It would help if she had an idea where they were. She could sense Chandler's hesitancy, so she asked the unspoken question. "Do we need to follow the tracks?"

"That will take us farther north and away from Liberty. I think we should travel west."

"Won't another train be coming through? Maybe it'd be better to stay close to the tracks."

He shook his head. "I don't know. It could be twenty-four hours before another train comes through. This land is fenced, which likely means there are cattle. Cattle means a rancher is someplace nearby."

"You're probably right. I want to get back on the road and find my boy."

"Josie knows we're in trouble and should send someone this way. Let's head west until we come to a road." He whistled. "Come on, Tucker."

Bristol followed behind the duo. "What about the engineer? Do you think they'll call in the crash?"

Chandler glanced toward the tunnel. "We'll know in a bit when we pass the tunnel."

"True." She guessed it was about seven at night, and they maybe had two hours of sunlight left. She hoped they found a ranch or road soon. Most of all, they needed a phone. Then they could get a ride back to town and let the authorities know where the kidnapper had last been seen.

A few minutes later, they came to the tunnel. The truck's bumper lay on the ground in a twisted mess, and on the side of the tunnel, broken pieces of glass and metal shone along the tracks.

Chandler said, "The rest of the truck must still be on the train."

"I was thinking the same thing." She shielded her eyes from the sun. The tracks curved up ahead, but the train was nowhere in sight. "Do you see the train?"

"No. It takes a long distance for one to stop. Did you hear the brakes?"

Bristol thought for a moment but couldn't recall any sound. "Not really, but I was busy jumping."

He nodded and then grimaced. Evidently, the pain was great.

She decided not to make him talk more. When she was in pain, the last thing she wanted to do was carry on a conversation. They wound their way through the trees until they ended in prairie grass.

Chandler stopped and surveyed their surroundings. He pointed. "This way."

They veered toward the left. In the distance, a power line came into view, and she figured they were close to a road. She spoke her thoughts out loud.

"That's what I was thinking, too."

Twenty minutes later, they reached the power poles, but still no road. Well, nothing you could call a road. A small path led to the perimeter of the fence, but it looked like they were still on private land.

Chandler slowed, and he'd stopped sweating a while ago.

"We can stop if you need to," she offered.

"I'm fine. Let's keep moving."

She did as he asked, but worry set in along with the sun. Blood stained his shirt, even though none of it looked fresh. He tried to appear strong, but he was fading. As much as she hated the thought, he was slowing her down.

If they didn't find help soon, what should she do? Go for help? Travel would be much quicker without him. Even as the thought came to her, guilt nagged at her for thinking of leaving him. She didn't like to admit it, but Chandler had been helpful and kind. Something she hadn't expected from him—or any man.

Every step was excruciating for Chandler, but he couldn't let Bristol know how badly his injury hindered him. The pain had to be ignored. He forced himself to take a step and then another. Maybe they should've followed the train tracks. They must've driven farther east while being chased than he'd realized. He was familiar with much of North Texas, but some areas were vast farms and ranches and sparsely populated.

Dallas, Houston and San Antonio continued to grow, but once a person got out of commuting distance, the areas thinned into farming communities. Another hour north would put them into Oklahoma. Tucker, his faithful companion, stayed a few feet in front of them, leading the way.

The sun would be down soon. They needed to find shelter and a phone before then. As much as his body begged for a reprieve, he couldn't take one.

Bristol powered on behind him without complaint. He didn't know her well except for the few things he'd heard during Rex's case. He wondered now about the lady. Why had she ever married Rex to begin with? Her love for Spencer was obvious, and she appeared to have her head on straight, not like a whimsical young lady. Chandler had dated plenty of those in high school and while at the academy. He'd never dated seriously but had gone from one short-term relationship to another. That was part of his dad's complaint—always asking when Chandler was going to settle down.

Even now, his mom often inquired about his "love life." Her desire for grandkids had never been a secret, but it had seemed to grow worse following his dad's disappearance. But after that day, Chandler had taken a good look at his life—at his choices. His dad had been right. Chandler went from day to day with no thought of the future. Sure, he'd gotten into law enforcement mainly because he had followed in his dad's footsteps, but he didn't know what else he wanted to do with his life. Unlike officers in the movies or on drama shows who had a calling to protect and serve, for Chandler, it just seemed like the thing to do. Fresh out of high school, he had no desire to go to college for four or more years and wasn't interested in a trade.

Suddenly, his boot hit something hard, and he tripped.

Bristol's hand shot out and grabbed his arm. "Whoa. That was a big rock."

Pain ran down his arm, and he brushed her away. "I've got it." Irritation seeped through him at his lack of energy. Ever since jumping from the train, his strength had drained away with each step. There was no time for rest. He simply had no choice but to keep going.

"There's something in those trees." She pointed. "A shed or house, maybe."

He forced himself to concentrate on the horizon. The setting sun reflected on something. "I see it."

As they trekked on, Tucker stopped and put his nose to the air and stared in the structure's direction.

"What is it, Tuck?" The canine glanced his way before trotting toward the building.

In the distance, a coyote howled, and Bristol stared in the direction of the sound. It'd be dark in thirty minutes.

Chandler pushed hard, trying to keep up. Pure determination was the only thing that kept him on his feet. To his right, water trickled in a narrow creek, and he was happy he didn't have to cross it. Several minutes later, they closed in on the place. As it came into better view, a pole shed covered in tin took shape. He glanced around but didn't see a house or shop. "There's nothing here."

"Let's search around to be sure."

Long shadows covered the ground, making it difficult to see, but he took careful steps, not wanting to trip again. A glance into the shed showed a horseshoe in the dirt and a couple of metal welding rods. A five-gallon bucket sat in the corner. Hoofprints marked the ground. As Bristol continued to look around, Chandler leaned heavily on one of the poles.

Tucker took off with his nose to the ground.

Against Chandler's will, weakness overtook him. He allowed his head to rest against the pole and his eyes closed. They needed to keep moving. He had to get Bristol to safety and contact his team. But his world grew darker. He forced his eyes open, and the darkening sky spun. And then he was falling.

He lay in the dirt, his eyes fixed on distant stars. If they didn't get help soon, they were in big trouble. And what would Bristol do alone?

NINE

Bristol's breath hitched as Tucker licked Chandler and whimpered. She hurried over and knelt. "Chandler?"

His cheek was cool to the touch. That was good. "Chandler, are you all right?" When he didn't answer, she tried again, giving him a shake. "Chandler, wake up."

He mumbled something but didn't move. The slow rise and fall of his chest said he was still breathing. Fear fell on her. She would be stuck out here all night, sitting and waiting, while her boy got farther away. Chandler needed medical care, and there was no way to reach anyone. Unless she kept moving.

Lord, what do I do? I need Your help. Please, keep Spencer and Chandler safe.

She'd never felt so alone before. The stars shone in the sky, and the full moon illuminated the area. Lazy clouds drifted overhead. A coyote howled somewhere. And then more joined in.

Tucker's ears went straight up as he stared into the distance.

Chills went down her arm. The shed was in a clearing among the trees. She had always enjoyed camping as a kid. Kirk Canfield had taken her and her mom camping several times. He was one of the few men Bristol had wished would've married her mom. He'd maintained a small ranch and even owned a couple of horses and had taught Bristol to ride.

Worry weighed heavy on her shoulders after another glance at Chandler. The need to keep moving and do something convinced her to build a fire. Even though it was late May, the night would grow cool before morning. Something moved in the bushes, and she jumped.

Her heart raced as she stared, trying to figure out who or what was out there. "Anybody there?"

Okay. Now she was being silly. If anyone was out there, she would've seen them. Tucker circled Chandler and then lay down beside him.

Must be nothing too important or the dog would be on alert. "Okay, boy, I'm going to gather wood for a fire."

Tucker rested his face on his paws, but his brown eyes followed her.

She had never been afraid of the dark, but she'd also never stayed the night outside or went camping all alone. Chandler was with her, but she felt the need to protect more than be protected. As she quickly gathered sticks in her arms, she was careful to stay close to Tucker. Surely he would warn her if a person or animal approached.

As she dropped the wood on the ground, the deputy stirred. Another brush of her fingers across his face showed he was still cool to the touch. The loss of blood must've exhausted him.

With a pile of dead leaves and a bit of decayed bark, she created kindling. Earlier, she'd seen Chandler fiddle with a lighter he kept in his back pocket. Carefully, she reached in. As her fingers touched the cloth, she bumped his gun, and his eyes shot open. His hand grabbed her arm as he half sat up.

"What are you doing?"

She jumped. "Going to start a fire."

His eyes bounced around, looking wild. He blinked before falling back against the earth. "I feel awful."

She removed the lighter and noticed the initials *SBM* engraved in bold font. What had the *S* and *B* stood for? Maybe it wasn't Chandler's. She ran her thumb down the tiny wheel and was relieved when the lighter sparked to life. Once a blaze was going, she added a few more thin sticks before adding two larger ones.

The sun had completely set now, and the stars and moon shone high in the sky. Smoke rose into the night air. Chandler appeared to have gone back to sleep. Since help wouldn't be coming soon, she needed to check his wound. Not that she had any medical training, but she could at least clean the injury. An infection would only make things more difficult, and she didn't think they could afford any more problems right now.

They'd passed a small creek a few yards back. She grabbed the bucket from the shed and then patted her thigh. "Come on, Tucker. Go with me."

He jumped to his feet and followed her the thirty yards to the water. The wind whistled through the trees and grass. Crickets chirped and frogs croaked in the distance, creating an unnerving sensation with the shadows and other nighttime sounds. Not wanting to waste time, she dipped the bucket into the shallow stream, allowing the water to seep in, and rinsed it out before filling it a quarter of the way full.

Tucker lapped from the stream. Poor boy must be tired and thirsty.

Rustling sounded somewhere nearby. Immediately,

Tucker went into a barking fit. Chills marched down her spine and she stepped back while lugging the water. A quick glance into the field showed several pairs of white eyes glowing in the darkness.

She continued to step back. "Come on, Tucker."

But he continued his barking tirade with his hackles raised.

"No." She reached out and grabbed his harness. He pulled hard against it. "No," she repeated. "Let's get back to Chandler."

She hurried to the clearing, running by the time she got there. Water splashed the side of her leg. Tucker continued to bark and stare into the field.

A coyote howled close by. Several more joined in.

Bristol shook off the shivers. Would the coyotes attack?

Chandler opened his eyes and moved to sit. He pushed up twice before he made it. "What's going on?"

She quickly explained about them reaching the shed and him falling asleep.

Another howl.

He glanced over his shoulder and then back to Tucker, whose hackles were raised again. "Come here, Tucker." He patted his leg. The dog lay next to him, but his head remained raised. "You don't want to go out there, boy."

"There's more than just one." At his questioning look, she continued, "I took Tucker to get some water so I could clean your injury. Not only are there several, but they're close. I've been around coyotes most of my life, but I've never seen them come this near before. Thing is, normally the beasts fear humans. These don't seem to be afraid."

"We'll keep the fire going. And, Bristol…"

"Yeah?"

"I'm sorry."

"No need." She ripped off a small strip of cloth from the bottom of her T-shirt and dipped it in the water before handing it to him. "Thought this might help."

He peeled back his shirt, and she could tell by his pained expression that his shirt must've stuck to the wound. He gently prodded the injury.

"Are you feeling better?"

He released a breath and, cupping his hands, drank from the bucket. In between sips, he said, "I can't remember being this weak before. But I'll get us back."

No. She'd get herself to somewhere safe. Bristol had learned a long time ago, dealing with Rex, that it was better to do her thing, but don't argue. If you argued, the guy would just put up a bigger fight. Maybe not all men were that way, but holding her tongue had served her well. She would bide her time and then go for help herself.

His gaze went to the woods before he attempted to stand. "I'll get more fuel for the fire."

She'd gotten plenty for the next couple of hours, although she didn't comment. Chandler made it to his feet but held on to the pole for balance.

"Are you certain you need to be up? You should probably sit down until your strength returns."

"I'm fine."

He took a step and then stopped. After a pause, he moved toward the trees.

"If you go down out there, I won't be able to get you close to the fire. You're much too big for me to drag."

He turned back to her, a smile lifting the side of his mouth. "That bad, huh?"

The gesture did something funny to her insides. He

certainly should show his pearly whites more often. "I'd say so."

To her surprise, he dropped back to the ground. "You can't give a guy a break, can you?"

"Not hardly. That macho man stuff doesn't impress me."

His grin widened. "Why doesn't that surprise me?" His face sobered like his thoughts had returned to reality. "We're in trouble here, Bristol."

"I know that." It took everything in her not to take off walking to find her son. The thought of him being out there and scared was almost more than she could stand.

"I'm certain you do. You look exhausted." Concern consumed his gaze. His fingers prodded his head. "Why don't you get some sleep? I'll keep watch."

She didn't trust him to stay awake. Oh, she knew he wanted to help, but she couldn't depend on him. "I'm fine. You're the one who has lost a lot of blood. You need to be in a hospital. Rest. By morning, I'd like to be moving again."

"No." He shook his head. "Stay awake if you wish, but I'm staying up, too. Besides the cut on my shoulder, I'm fine. No bumps on the head that I could find."

Fine. She couldn't make him rest. He was just as stubborn as she was. The grass grew wet with dew, and the night turned chilly. Without a blanket and in a T-shirt, she wrapped her arms around herself. Tucker lay next to Chandler, but she wished the dog would bring his warmth to her.

She tossed a couple more sticks on the fire, making sparks pop into the sky, and moved even closer. The heat felt good.

Worry continued to lie heavy in her heart, making her stomach ache. Where was Spencer? Was he all right? No matter how much she told herself he was fine, she didn't know that. Why did someone want a three-year-old boy, anyway? Revenge? To sell him?

There were no good scenarios.

The only positive thing was the suspect wasn't trying to kill her at the moment. He was long gone. Which brought up another question. Where did the men plan on taking Spencer?

A twig snapped, and her head jerked toward the sound.

Three pairs of glowing white eyes shone against the darkness.

"Chandler, we have company."

"I see that."

Silhouettes moved, and one at a time, the mangy coyotes drew closer to the fire. Tucker leaped to his feet and growled.

Right now, Bristol thought, she would rather take her chances with their kidnapper. "Chandler…" Her voice came out high-pitched against her will. "Do something."

Chandler put his hand on the ground and got to his feet. He drew his gun and aimed.

The closest beast leaped, and Chandler fired, the shot going wide. A piece of his Glock fell to the ground.

She blinked at the broken gun.

Fear settled in her chest as she watched him toss it at the coyote. He was too weak to fend off the beasts alone. They were going to have to work as a team.

Chandler wavered on his feet even as he concentrated on staying upright. "Get behind me."

Bristol grabbed a stick and moved to his side.

One of the coyotes, a large, rangy male with a scar down his nose, moved closer. Gray lined his muzzle, declaring he was old and experienced. At least two more animals stayed back from the light, but Chandler could make out their movements. He wasn't certain if his eyes were playing tricks on him or not, but he thought several younger beasts watched from the grass.

Tucker took a few steps toward the coyotes and barked in a fury.

"Heel, Tuck. Heel."

His companion continued to sound the alarm but moved beside him.

No matter what, Chandler couldn't afford to go down and leave Bristol to defend herself. She'd be alone then, and the animals would sense victory.

One of the logs spit sparks, but the end of it rested on the ground, and he picked it up. "Get back. Back!"

The rangy leader paced back and forth on the other side of the flames, his gaze bouncing between Chandler and Bristol. While this one commanded attention, Chandler didn't let his guard down with the others. Even though he'd never been stalked by animals, he knew coyotes were mostly solitary animals but would hunt together, yelping and scaring their prey out of the bushes. When the rabbits or other prey ran from the noise, they'd all attack. He had known coyotes to take down larger animals, like a sick cow or one that had just given birth.

Chandler raised the stick, and those yellow-whitish eyes penetrated the darkness. He grabbed another log and held it out to Bristol. "Take this. If one of them gets close, don't hesitate to strike."

She took the log and dropped the other one into the flames.

One of the younger coyotes circled behind them and charged, snipping and yelping.

"Chandler!" She turned and swung, and the coyote jumped back.

Tucker swiveled, barking and growling. He leaped forward, and Chandler barely grabbed his harness in time. "Heel. Heel, Tucker." Never had he witnessed his dog so aggressive, but he supposed the bloodhound was acting on instinct.

In his peripheral vision, he saw several more coyotes move in.

He needed to do something or they'd be surrounded. The leader continued to make his way closer. Chandler repositioned his grip on the stick and took a step forward. He swung the limb like a baseball bat, the rangy one dodging the attempt. Chandler's momentum carried him around, and he dropped to one knee before shoving back to both feet.

His gaze remained steady on the big one.

"Oh, no, you don't." Bristol struck out with her stick, sparks dropping onto the ground.

Chandler snatched another long, wispy stick from the fire and stepped toward the animals. At least five paced in the shadows but continually drew closer. The big one snarled, making the hair on the back of Chandler's neck stand up.

A skinny female suddenly rushed in on his left, and out of reflex, Chandler struck out. The tip of the stick connected, and she yelped. Two coyotes advanced, and he swung both arms, sparks flinging into the grass like sparklers on the Fourth of July. A small tuft of grass went up in flames.

With all the movement, dizziness threatened to overtake him. Tucker continued to growl, and one of the wild beasts bounded at them, nipping at Tucker's hind end.

His bloodhound spun and snapped.

"Don't let them get Tucker!" Bristol screeched. She stepped out and swung as hard as she could. The stick connected with a young coyote, and another yelp was her reward.

So far, the animals were not hurt, but they weren't in as much of a hurry to attack, either.

The rangy one suddenly sprang at Chandler.

"No!" Bristol screamed.

The animal's teeth dug into the flesh of his arm. Automatically, he jerked, trying to dislodge the hold. The stick in that hand dropped to the ground. He swung the other limb, and the flames extinguished. The tip must've been hot, for the rangy thing released his hold.

Tucker snapped at the coyote, but the wild animal darted through the grass and disappeared.

The skinny female yelped a few times and then they all ran off. And then all was quiet.

Chandler glanced down at Tucker, his head high and his tail in the air, still alert.

"Are you all right?" Bristol retained her grip on her stick.

"I'm fine." But that wasn't true. The stars melted into the blackness. While he was still on his feet, he found his gun in the grass and returned to the fire.

"Sit down before you fall."

"I'm not going to fall." But he dropped to the ground anyway. He scooped up the slide lock that had fallen from the gun and examined it. Sure enough, the lock spring had broken. If he had a spare with him, he could repair the Glock in five minutes. He shoved the gun back into his holster, seeing it was useless for now.

Tucker whimpered and paced around the campfire, constantly glancing back into the night. Whether he could see the animals or not, Chandler didn't know.

Bristol came and sat beside him with her back toward the shed. "We've got to do something."

"I agree with you." His arm burned like crazy from where the coyote got him. He was certain the few stitches the paramedics had put in had reopened. From his arm being stabbed, to the hard landing from jumping from the train, and now this, he needed medical care. And in the back of his mind, Spencer was getting farther away.

"Let me see your arm."

He turned his arm so she could see. "I don't think it's deep, but it burns."

She grimaced. "Ouch. That looks like it hurts." Her fingers gently prodded the bite wound. "Did you get stitches earlier?"

"I did after you left the crash site."

"Hmm. Doesn't look like they pulled out. I think you're right, though. Looks like a superficial injury. You need some antibiotic cream and a doctor to look at you."

"I agree." He nodded.

"I should go for help." Her words came out soft and noncombative.

"No way. We stick together." What was the lady thinking? As if he'd let her be out there on her own. If she'd been away from the fire when the animals attacked, she couldn't have gotten away.

"Chandler, I appreciate your care. I know you were trained to protect me, and I understand that. But I need to find my son, and I can't just sit here. I've been thinking. If the shed is here, there's bound to be a ranch close. Those hoofprints belong to someone's cattle. I spent a little time on a ranch myself, learned to ride a horse, and know that the animals must be checked on and cared for. This is the calving season. People don't just leave the animals without checking on them. I will head due south and follow the power lines. Keep Tucker here with you by the fire. I'll call authorities, and help will be here before morning."

He squinted as he looked at her. Her tone remained light and easy. Was she always this matter-of-fact? He got the feeling she was trying to manipulate him. Most women he knew would put their foot down, including his mom, sister and aunts. "Are you kidding me?"

"What?"

He shook his head. There was no need to quibble, because she was acting easy to get along with, but he didn't buy the act. She carried a gun and didn't appear helpless. She'd turned her drug-dealing husband in to the authorities—something that must've put her in danger. "Never mind."

She opened her mouth, as if to argue, but then swallowed down the words.

His body had never been so utterly weak in his life, and he hated it. He had to keep going. Unless he was unconscious, he wasn't about to let Bristol go off without protection. He hadn't taken seriously his mom's concerns over his dad, and then he'd disappeared. Chandler had learned his lesson. Bristol's safety was his responsibility, and he intended to watch over her, even if it killed him.

"Come on—let's go." He motioned to her. She stepped beside him. "So you lived on a ranch and rode horses?"

She nodded. "Just for a little while. My mom's fiancé taught me to ride. You should rest. You're injured. Even though you try to hide it, I can see you're in pain and are struggling."

"Thanks for the sympathy, but I'll be the judge of

when I need to rest." He didn't look at her but patted his thigh. "Come on, Tucker."

The dog jumped to his feet and wagged his tail.

She didn't respond, but he had the feeling if he turned around, he'd see her shooting daggers at him with her eyes.

TEN

Bristol helped Chandler kick dirt over the campfire before they headed south. They wove through the trees until it broke into open land. Without saying a word, Chandler stuck close to the power lines, like she'd suggested.

She didn't know how he stayed on his feet. Stubborn man. His energy seemed zapped, and if they came upon trouble again, like the coyotes or their attackers, he'd be a goner. But he was trying to help, and that was endearing in her book. Growing up moving from town to town, she hadn't established roots long enough to have anyone stand up for her. Once she was in middle school, she quit trying to make friends. Why get close if you knew you were going to lose them?

She didn't know why she'd mentioned riding horses to Chandler. Kirk Canfield was the only man her mom had dated whom Bristol had grown close to. He'd spent time with Bristol, letting her help on his ranch and teaching her to ride. Most of her mom's love interests sent Bristol away or wanted to leave her with a sitter. But not Kirk. He'd proposed to her mom just a month before the accident.

Kirk had taken Bristol out for a ride that October afternoon. He was on a four-year-old black horse named Midnight who loved to run—so much so the horse required an experienced rider, or the animal would run off. Bristol was on Emma, a gentle eleven-year-old palomino. But as they were galloping across the open pasture with Bristol in the lead, Emma's back foot tangled in some discarded hay-bale twine, and she got spooked. She reared up, causing Bristol to drop the reins. The palomino barreled toward the trees with her clinging to the saddle horn. Several limbs smacked Bristol, but she hung on for dear life. Bristol had only been riding for a few months and didn't know what to do. Kirk shot into action and quickly caught up to them in the woods. But as they came out on the other side of the trees, Midnight almost ran smack-dab into a pickup pulling a cattle trailer on a rock road. The horse startled and tossed his head. Kirk was thrown into the road. The pickup was able to dodge Kirk by hitting the ditch, but the trailer struck him.

The driver called 9-1-1, and an EMS helicopter flew him to the hospital some sixty miles away. After he spent two weeks in the trauma unit for a spine injury, it was determined Kirk would never walk again.

A sideways glance showed Chandler's set jaw and furrowed brow as he trekked through the tall grass—determination radiating like the Texas sun in the middle of July. Inwardly, she sighed. As much as she appreciated his help, he was actually weighing her down. If she still had her gun, she might consider going on without him. That wasn't an option.

If the roles were reversed and she was the one injured, would she have stayed to help him? No way. Guilt tugged at her for the admission. Was he for real? She'd met few people who had taken an interest in helping others. She'd gotten so independent and only worried about her and Spencer, which was the way it needed to be.

The real nightmare of losing her son forever was staring her in the face, and she didn't know how to stop it. Her stomach remained in one continuous knot. Even the night she'd run from Rex, hoping and praying to get away, hadn't been as frightening as her son disappearing.

She didn't care about revenge. Or even justice. All she wanted was her son back.

How did parents of missing children survive? Well, she wasn't going to find out, because she'd find Spencer if it was the last thing she did. The thought made her wonder about Chandler. What made him join Bring the Children Home Project? He'd never mentioned children or a wife. He also didn't wear a wedding ring— something she couldn't help but notice on a man ever since she'd been married to Rex. She often wondered if all men were like her ex and flirted or chased other women. So far, Chandler had done neither.

She said another prayer like she'd done repeatedly since she'd received the call from the daycare.

As the grass grew taller, she watched her step and was thankful for the moonlight. Her gaze stayed glued to the back of Chandler's shirt as she walked in his path. It was good Tucker was with them to warn of trouble.

Somewhere a cow bawled, followed by another.

They trekked across the open pasture for what seemed like forever but was probably only fifteen or twenty minutes. Except for the occasional stumble, Chandler continued with minor problems.

A barbed-wire fence stretched across the horizon. "Looks like that might be a road."

"Yeah." Chandler's eyes narrowed. He pointed to the south. "Is that a barn?"

A security light shone in the distance, but Bristol couldn't tell what the buildings were. "I hope whoever lives there is awake and has a phone."

He didn't respond but picked up the pace a bit.

What if the suspect or his accomplice lived there? Or this was their hideout?

Tucker trotted happily in front of them, and he stuck his nose to the ground as they drew closer. Occasionally, he'd stop and sniff the air.

Headlights appeared in the distance on the road.

"Someone's headed this way, and they're driving fast. Let's move."

They hurried into the yard, and Bristol jogged up the porch steps. She knocked on the door. No sounds came from inside the house, but a horse whinnied from the barn.

Chandler stepped up behind her and banged harder. "Hello?" When no one answered, he gave the knob a try, and the door swung inward.

A dark flatbed truck slowed in front of the house.

Chandler gave her a little push. "Hurry. Run to the barn and take Tucker with you. I'm going to see if there's a phone to call for help. I'll join you in a bit. If I'm not there in five minutes, hide."

Bristol hurried around the side of the house, careful to stay out of the headlights as the truck pulled into the drive. "Come on, Tuck."

The dog trotted beside her.

The west side of the barn had an open cattle pen, and she hustled under the overhang and glanced back. More than likely the driver was the owner of the home, but she was concerned about Chandler. What if they caught him inside the home? They'd think he was robbing the place.

The low rumble of the engine slowed as the driver stopped in the front yard.

She entered the barn through a side door and allowed her eyes to grow accustomed to the darkness before moving deeper in. A horse stamped his foot from a stall, and she moved closer, hoping to find a suitable hiding place. The horse was beautiful and big—an Appaloosa. She swallowed. Tragic memories flooded her mind. She hadn't been near a horse in years.

There were two stalls, but the other one was piled with hay bales. A pitchfork leaned against the railing, and she took it.

The sound of the barn door opening and shutting had her dropping to her knee on the straw-covered ground. She pulled Tucker close to her chest and wrapped her free arm around his neck. Any sound or whimper might give her position away.

Footsteps moved across the open space, and her grip tightened on the pitchfork.

"Bristol, it's me," Chandler whispered.

She stood and motioned. "Over here."

He hurried to her side and knelt on the ground, a rifle in his hand. "There are two guys. Neither was the one who drove the maroon truck."

"Where did you get the gun?"

"I found it and a box of ammo in a bedroom closet."

She leaned closer. "Did you see Spencer?"

"No, but I was in a hurry to get out of there."

Her stomach clenched at the uncertainty of what was happening to him. Not that she thought her son would come running out, but still. Where were they keeping him? "Do you think the men are the landowners?"

She leaned close, and Tucker's tail thumped against the ground as he sniffed Chandler.

"Not unless they'd been out hunting. Both were carrying guns. One guy looked like the one who drove the white BMW, but it's difficult to tell in the dark. I didn't exactly have time to hang around." He kept his voice low. "I didn't find a landline, just the gun."

She nodded.

A voice rose from outside. "Check every building. They're here. There's fresh blood on the floor."

Bristol froze. She didn't recognize either voice. Was Chandler bleeding again?

Chandler peeked outside through a window. "They're lighting a makeshift torch."

Tucker jumped to his feet and barked.

"Shh, boy." Chandler patted the dog on the head, but it was too late.

One of the men said, "The barn."

The other one yelled, "Come on out and make this easy. We know you're in there."

He grabbed the sleeve of her T-shirt, pulling her closer. "Ride west parallel to the road. Stop at the first house you come to and call Josie."

Bristol hunkered lower. "Not on the horse. I'll go on foot."

"No time for that. Take the horse." He whispered, but urgency laced his words. "I'm going to create a diversion, and I want you to run for it."

She shook her head. "No…"

"Bristol, no time to argue. We need help so we can find Spencer. Now." He hurried to the horse. "Come on. I'll give you a boost."

Visions of Kirk Canfield being thrown from Midnight ran through her mind, giving her chills.

"I don't ride." Anymore.

"You don't have a choice." Chandler's face grew red as he grabbed a bridle from a hook on the wall and slid it on the Appaloosa.

"I always have a choice." She shoved her shoulders back. "I make my own decisions."

As he went for the saddle, she repeated, "I don't ride."

"Yes, you do. I remember you talked about riding horses when you lived on some ranch. Even if it's been a while, you must ride."

But she'd told no one about Kirk. About how she could never get the image of him flying off that horse out of her head. How after Kirk spent months in rehab, her mom had walked away from the man. And the father figure of Bristol's dreams was no more.

When she was older and got her driver's license, she'd finally gotten up the resolve to go see her mom's ex-fiancé. She needed to apologize. But when she pulled into his drive and saw the wheelchair ramp to his front door, she'd turned around and left.

She feared she'd receive payback for never telling Kirk how she felt.

Chandler handed the reins to her. "I'll wait until you're out of the barn door before I start shooting."

"No." Panic filled her. She couldn't...

He glanced out the door. "They're headed this way. You must do it, Bristol." His gaze softened. "Your little boy is depending on you."

She swallowed hard. Of course, he was right. But what if she froze like she'd done while riding Emma? Or the countless times Rex had threatened her? Bristol was better off keeping away from trouble than she was facing it head-on.

Her breath slipped away, and she struggled to bring

it under control. "I've taken shooting lessons. I'd rather take on the bad guys."

"Bristol, I've got a plan, but there's no time to explain." His eyes grew large with impatience. "Ride out of here."

One man darted behind the trees, flames burning from a torch in his hand.

"They're coming." He gave her a push. "Go!"

She took the reins and stepped into the saddle. *Please, God, help me. I don't want to do this.*

With his hands on the harness, Chandler led her to the side door. "Don't look back. Just keep going. Tucker and I will catch up to you later."

Her heart hitched at the concern in his eyes, and then he slapped the Appaloosa on the rump. "Yaw!"

The horse jumped and took off at a run. Bristol not only held the reins, but she clutched the saddle horn just in case she dropped the reins.

Pop. Pop. Pop.

Gunfire sounded behind her, and she started to look back but stopped herself. *Do what Chandler said.* It would be all right. He wouldn't steer her wrong.

Out of her peripheral vision, flames flittered in the wind. She dug her heels into the horse's flanks and he ran even faster, eating up the ground. She didn't dodge a scraggly bush but plowed over it and kept going. Cattle scattered as they galloped through the grazing herd.

Boom! An explosion rocked the ground.

The Appaloosa whinnied and bucked.

"No!" Bristol gripped the reins tighter, and her legs squeezed hard into his sides. "It's okay, boy."

But the animal threw his head up and went back on his hind legs. She grabbed the saddle horn and slithered to the back of the seat. Her foot slid through the stirrup, causing her to slide toward the left.

Fear assaulted her, making her world spin. The horse was going to throw her! She couldn't fall.

Finally, his front feet pounded the ground, and he took off again. He put his head down and bolted across the open pasture. She tried to slow him, but it was no use. The animal was frightened, and she couldn't control him.

The moon shone brightly, but they were going too fast with no trail. She feared the horse would fall after he dodged brush and the ground dipped. A country road appeared on her right with nothing but a barbed-wire fence to separate them. She tugged the reins to the left, but the horse refused and continued straight on his course.

"Turn, boy. Turn."

The Appaloosa whinnied and didn't slow. Didn't he see the fence?

He was going to jump it. They'd never make it. It was too high, and the ditch was steep on the other side.

A rumble of an engine sounded from behind, but she was barely aware of it. "Whoa, boy."

"Bristol. Slow down."

Chandler? His voice called to her, but didn't he understand she couldn't stop? The engine must've scared the horse, for he veered away from the fence.

A narrow creek crossed the pasture, and as they approached, Bristol pulled back harder on the reins. "Whoa. Whoa."

The horse must've seen it, for he leaped across to the other side in a single action. The flatbed truck roared behind her. She glanced over her shoulder in time to see the truck precariously tilt and then climb up the other side.

The horse tired, and his neck lathered under the effort. At the bottom of the valley, a ravine split the land wide-open. This was much too broad for them to jump.

She pulled on the reins and leaned back in the stirrups, but the horse tugged his head lower, fighting against her. Chandler drew closer. She waved her hand. "Get back!"

Chandler was going to do a nosedive into the ravine. She couldn't bear to see him get hurt like Kirk. Not to save her. Without thinking of the consequence, she threw her leg over the saddle. Another person would not ruin his life because of her.

Not Chandler. The man had done everything in his power to help her.

Chandler was shocked as he saw Bristol jump off the horse. His chest tightened. He hit his brakes, sending his truck sideways. The front end dipped into the ravine, but he couldn't stop. The truck slid down the embankment and slammed into the bottom. His head snapped forward from the force.

He slung open his door and ran to where Bristol lay on the ground, her body contorted in a tangled mess. "Are you all right?"

A moan escaped her, and she twisted into a ball.

"Bristol, it's me. Chandler. Where do you hurt?"

Her eyes locked on to his, and she blinked. "Everywhere."

A smile tugged at his lips, relief flooding him. Tucker appeared beside them and sniffed Bristol, checking her out.

Chandler gently touched her shoulder. "We only have a little time before those guys catch up to us."

"Are you...?" She gasped. "Were you hurt? There was an explosion."

She was concerned about *him*? "I'm fine."

"You crashed into the ravine. I couldn't bear..."

Worry settled back into his throat. Maybe she was more injured than he believed. Might have hit her head. "I'm not hurt."

"The horse. What about the Appaloosa?"

He glanced up and saw the horse standing on this side of the ravine, his chest rising and falling and slicked up with lather. "The horse is not harmed."

A look at the suspects' truck had him wondering if he'd be able to get it out of the ditch. If not, they'd be on foot. A place he didn't want to be if those guys got back on their trail. And no doubt, they would pursue them again, if they weren't already.

Her eyes closed, almost like in sleep. If it weren't for the scrapes and dirt-covered arms, she wouldn't appear injured.

"Bristol, can you move?"

Her eyes fluttered open.

"Those guys are still after us. We need to find Spencer."

"Spencer. I'm ready." She sat up and struggled to her feet, weaving.

He held on to her arm until she got her balance.

"Do I need to get back on the horse?"

"Let me see if I can get the truck out." He turned to move, but her hand shot out.

"No. Here they come." She nodded, indicating the top of the hill. The two men ran toward them.

The truck's front tire was buried halfway up the side.

It was possible he could get it out…but maybe not. "Let me see if I can catch the horse."

He whistled lightly. "Here, boy."

As he approached, the horse jerked his head up, his ears perked. The reins were caught on a branch. *Please don't run off.* He stepped closer, and footsteps sounded behind him.

Bristol moved past him. "I can catch him."

A quick look over his shoulder showed the men were closing in on them. "We need to hurry."

"I've got you." Bristol reached out and grabbed the bridle and then pulled on the reins until they were free of the limb. She went to put her foot in the stirrup, when she swayed.

Chandler picked her up and swung her into the saddle, his injured arm burning from the effort. Then he climbed on behind and took the reins from her. "Come on, Tucker."

Gunshots sounded and kicked up the dirt at the horse's feet. Chandler glanced over his shoulder. The two men had stopped and aimed a rifle.

Chandler kicked the horse, and they took off up the hill. The Appaloosa had already ridden hard and fast, so Chandler didn't cherish riding him again, but there simply wasn't a choice until they were out of gun range. Tucker ran behind them.

Bristol leaned forward, evidently trying to give him more room, but space only made riding double more dangerous. With the reins in his right hand, his left arm went around her waist. He didn't trust she hadn't been injured when she jumped off the horse.

After about a quarter of a mile, they rode down the other side of the hill and into green spring grass and grazing cattle. The men were only a half mile behind them. If they continued their pursuit and didn't stop for their truck, it wouldn't take long.

As they topped the next hill, a small clapboard house came into view. A security light shone on the side yard. Two pickup trucks sat in the drive.

"Those aren't the same ones that chased us, are they?"

"I sure hope not." He rubbed the back of his neck. "But we'll soon find out."

ELEVEN

Chickens clucked and scattered as she and Chandler rode into the yard. He slid off the horse and held his hand up to her to help her down.

A couple of dogs barked. The Appaloosa trotted to the cover of the trees and disappeared into the shadows.

After dealing with the coyotes, Bristol prepared for trouble, but two collie mix dogs rushed toward them, yapping up a storm.

"It's okay." Chandler talked in a friendly tone. "We're nice. Yeah, that's it. Good dogs."

They quit their racket and jogged up to them. Tucker and the collies circled and sniffed one another, checking each other out.

Bristol petted the one closer to her, when suddenly Chandler's hand shot out, stopping her.

"What is it?" She stared at him and noticed he looked toward the house.

"Who goes there?"

She glanced up to see a bare-chested man in jeans holding a shotgun pointed their way.

"We don't want trouble. I'm a Jarvis County deputy and need help."

The man lowered his weapon. "Come here, Dillon and Duke." The two dogs ran to the porch. As they approached, a woman in her bathrobe moved behind the man.

Chandler stayed back several yards and retained his grip on Tucker's harness. "We need to use a phone if you have one."

The woman said, "You're hurt. Come on in."

The man glanced at her but said nothing.

"We can wait outside." Chandler nodded. "We don't mind."

"Did you say you were a deputy?" the man asked.

"Yes, sir. Deputy Murphy."

The man's eyes squinted. "Murphy. Any kin to Simon Murphy?"

"He was my father."

The man stared a couple of seconds, scrutinizing him, before jerking his head. "Come on in. You can wait inside until help arrives. Or I can give you a ride somewhere."

"I appreciate this." Chandler glanced at Bristol and whispered, "Stay outside."

Okay. What was that look for? Did he detect danger? "I'll wait right here with Tucker."

The woman said, "Are you certain? It'd be warmer inside."

"I'm fine." Bristol offered a smile. "We've been walking, so I'm not cold." After the woman gave her another glance, they disappeared into the house. The main door remained open, but a screen door separated them.

Bristol's arms were a little cool, but Chandler had acted weird. Was he suspicious? Did he recognize this man, or was there something else?

She sat on the wooden steps, her feet killing her. Tucker lay beside her while the other two dogs continued to trot around the yard, sniffing and running back and forth to them. Tucker must be as exhausted as she was.

Chandler's voice carried to her as he gave the address to the small ranch but didn't elaborate on how they'd gotten there. A couple of minutes later, he returned outside, with the man following.

"I appreciate the help."

Bristol stood as Chandler joined her on the porch.

The man had put on a T-shirt that had seen its better days. "Like I said, I don't mind taking you into town."

"That's all right. We'll wait. Sorry to have woken you folks up." Chandler headed across the yard and turned to her. "Josie is on her way."

She hurried to catch up to his side. After they were out of hearing range, she asked, "What was all that about?"

He glanced back as if he was afraid they were being followed. He kept his voice down. "I recognize that man. It's been a few years, but the department investigated and arrested his son for selling drugs. Neil. That's his son's name. It was his first offense, but he got two years. The family didn't have money for a good lawyer. My dad was the investigator."

She glanced back over her shoulder at the house. The front door remained open. "Do you think he is behind the attacks?"

"Not really. But I don't want to take any chances."

"Hmm. Not a reassuring situation to be a deputy in the boonies needing help. Might give someone with a grudge a great opportunity."

"My thoughts exactly."

Chandler was relieved when two headlights approached them on the country road, and he recognized

Josie Hunt's Ford Bronco. Josie not only worked at Bring the Children Home Project but was also a private investigator.

He and Bristol had walked another two miles or more since leaving the small ranch. He'd half expected to have trouble with the couple since they may've had an axe to grind with his dad, and this presented an easy opportunity.

"Need a ride?" Josie said through her driver's-side window.

"You're a sight for sore eyes."

Bristol glanced his way before opening the door to the back seat.

"Wait." He held his hand up. The jacked-up, classic off-road SUV wasn't the easiest to crawl into. "Take the front. Tucker and I will get in the back."

She didn't argue but hurried around to the front. After they climbed into the vehicle, Bristol shook off the chill. "That wind made me cold."

Josie flicked up the heat and turned the vent toward her passenger. Then she glanced at Chandler in the rearview mirror. "What's going on?"

He went into the abbreviated version of the attack that forced them onto the train and then about the coyotes.

"Do you need to go to the hospital?"

"No. I'm feeling better and should be fine."

Josie gave him another look in the mirror. "What now?"

Bristol interjected, "We need to find Spencer. And I'm certain the deputy does need medical help."

"I'm good," he hurried to say. He would be checked out sometime today, but not first thing since he was feeling better.

The dashboard lights reflected on Josie's face as she glanced in the mirror again. "We don't know where your son is or who took him. Right?"

"Rex Edwards, my ex, was behind it."

Josie did a good job of not overreacting. "But he's dead. You think he paid someone to abduct your son before he died and had already put things in motion?"

"Yeah, I do. I know it sounds far-fetched, but there's no one else who would benefit from taking my son."

"Are you certain?"

"Yeah." Irritation radiated from Bristol's tone. "He's just a kid. Not a witness to a crime or something that would make someone come after him. Just a sweet little boy who goes to daycare, scribbles on his artwork and still runs to me for help if he scrapes his knee."

"I get what you're saying."

Chandler detected the despair in Bristol's voice, and it hurt him. He'd felt that way when he lost his dad. How much worse would it be to lose a child, someone you were supposed to protect?

Almost an hour later, they pulled into the sheriff's station. He walked around to the driver's side of the SUV. "Thanks, Josie."

"You're welcome. Keep in touch. I'll keep following leads as soon as I grab a few winks."

"You got it." After she pulled away, he and Bristol went inside. She made herself comfortable in the compact lobby. While he filled in Deputy Joyner, who was manning the office, Tucker trotted to Chandler's desk. The dog lapped water and nibbled on his food before lying down on the doggy bed.

Chandler filled out part of his paperwork and would finish during daytime hours—only a couple of hours away. He left his Glock to be repaired at the weapons armory and checked out another gun identical to his own, complete with plenty of ammunition.

When he entered the lobby, Deputy Joyner looked up. "We got a call from the railroad department about your truck. Seems it was smashed good, and they had it hauled to the impound lot."

"I'm sure the sheriff will love to hear that." Chandler would need to stop by sometime and get his things out of it.

Joyner nodded. "Yeah, the sheriff seems on edge lately."

Chandler had noticed that, too, and wondered if there was more going on that he didn't know about. Sometimes the mayor or city council came down on the leaders of law enforcement. Maybe that was what was bothering him. But Anthony's words returned to him about Sheriff Carroll asking about his dad's body. Had the sheriff been fishing for information or had there been something behind the question?

He walked over to Bristol. "Where would you like me to take you?"

Bristol blinked at him. "My car is wrecked, and your truck got demolished by the train tunnel. It's too early to rent a car."

"The department has a spare I can use."

"I suppose you can drop me off at my house, and I'll rent something as soon as the rental place opens. I'd rather get back on the abductor's trail before it goes cold."

He felt the same way. A terrible headache pounded behind his temples, but he tried to shove the pain to the back of his mind. What he really wanted to do was investigate this case a little deeper, but not with Bristol hanging around. It put her in too much danger, which was a distraction. "It's no problem to drop you off."

She got to her feet, looking dissatisfied. "Okay. I'd appreciate it."

"Come on, Tucker." Guilt weighed on him for not wanting her around while he worked the case. They walked out of the station to the spare car and climbed in, Tucker bounding into the back seat. He hated leaving Bristol, but he needed alone time to think.

"I'd like to get a phone first, no matter how cheap."

"Okay. There's not much open, but that large truck stop on the main highway has electronics."

"That'll work."

After they made a stop at the mega gas station/convenience store, where each of them bought a burner phone, she gave him the address to her house. He was familiar with the rural area and headed that way. Bristol was still quiet, and he resisted the need to fill the silence. Years ago, he had been boisterous and always joking and cutting up. Not obnoxious, but even then, he realized people enjoyed being around him. Confidence had never been an issue. He didn't have problems getting a date or having someone to hang out with. But after his dad disappeared, that all changed.

Now he wondered if he was making the right decision. Was he neglecting a clue, or was he just plain incompetent? His parents had warned him, but he had taken nothing seriously until disaster struck. Even his mom's desire for Chandler to quit the force made him doubt his ability to be a good deputy.

Now, most days, Chandler went straight home after work, even working cases at night. He took life more seriously and realized it could change in the blink of an eye. If he'd just asked his dad what was going on, his death could've been avoided.

Fifteen minutes later, Chandler pulled down a long rock drive. The modest older stone house sat in the valley with several trees scattered around, giving it a quaint, country welcome. He saw cattle grazing on the horizon of the pink sky. Nice place. How could she afford this while going to college?

"I rent it from a lady in the nursing home."

"What?"

"I see you're looking the place over. I prefer a rural setting, if possible, even though I've lived a little bit of everywhere, from apartments to a tiny RV with a leaky roof. Spencer needs fresh air. Mrs. Graham is not ready to give up her house yet and has hopes of moving back in after rehabilitation. I will admit, after months of her having therapy, I wonder if she will get better. When I first moved here, I stayed in an RV behind the main home until she went to the assisted-living place and her son sold the trailer. A neighbor leases the pasture for his cattle."

"Bristol, I wasn't trying to butt in."

"I could see the questions in your expression."

He wished he could convince her to let her defenses down, but it wouldn't matter once he found Spencer and brought down his kidnapper. It wasn't right, but disappointment that Rex was already dead plagued Chandler. He had wanted the man to pay for his father's death.

Vengeance is mine, I will repay, saith the Lord. The Scripture he'd heard most of his childhood popped into his mind, and shame filled him. It wasn't like he'd wished death upon Rex, but Chandler wanted justice.

Would Chandler ever learn the truth about what had happened to his father? Or would it be one of the unsolved cold cases whose evidence collected dust in a warehouse somewhere?

Not knowing was almost unbearable.

No matter what, he intended to make certain the same thing didn't happen to Bristol.

As her hand reached for the handle, he said, "Let me check the place out first."

"I've gotten pretty good at surveying my own place, but feel free to join the party."

He got out with her and attached Tucker's leash. The bloodhound leaped out and trotted along beside him. A light hung on the front of the house, illuminating the porch and part of the front yard. There was no security light, but as they stepped closer to the stone walk, a bulb in the corner of the house clicked on. And then the other corner.

Bristol removed something from the doorknob and then quickly punched in a number on a combination lock on the front door. His gaze took in the camera that was aimed down at him. He was glad she'd taken it upon herself to keep safe. So many people overlooked things like security when on a tight budget. But being married to Rex had probably taught her to be careful.

A quick walk through the house with Tucker at his side showed two bedrooms. The main bedroom had two beds—a queen in the middle and a twin pushed against the wall. The smaller one was covered in a tractor blanket. It appeared Spencer slept in this room. While there, Bristol grabbed another pistol from a wall safe high in the closet. She held a .45 in the air and then put it in a holster at her waistband. "I bought my first gun after leaving Rex at a pawnshop, but it was a little big. When I could afford it, I bought the nine-millimeter."

"Makes sense." The smaller bedroom contained a

wide variety of toys, from stuffed animals to metal farm tractors complete with plows and a barn. Spencer must have gotten used to sleeping in his mother's room or she didn't want the boy out of her sight. Probably the latter. Evidently, she had good reason to be concerned.

After a complete walk around and not seeing anything amiss, he turned to her. "Everything looks clear. You have any concerns?"

"Um, no. I think I got it." She gripped what looked to be a green-and-yellow pajama shirt in her hand and moved it away from her face. Had she been smelling the item of clothing?

Tucker moved to her side as if he sensed her distress.

Chandler stared at her. "You okay?"

"Fine." She dropped the pajamas to her side. "I have it under control."

"Hey." He stepped closer and took her hand. "We'll bring your son home."

Her lip trembled as she pulled away from his touch. "I know."

He was a mere couple of inches from her face, and one look into those blue eyes confirmed she was doing everything in her power to maintain control. He wished he could take away her pain, her worry. Without thinking, he leaned in and their gazes connected.

Tucker barked, and suddenly she stepped back.

He did the same, surprised he'd been tempted to kiss her. What had he been thinking?

"I appreciate the help, but I have my system down. I check the house and the barn." She talked like the awkward moment hadn't happened. "There are certain things I have in place that if moved, I'll know someone has been here."

"Like?"

"Sticky tape on the doorknob. I check the security camera before I lock up. And I have a bell on the barn door. If the door is opened, the bell falls. Not sophisticated, but it works. One time some neighboring teens played around in the barn."

"Did they steal anything?"

Her eyes glanced heavenward. "No. They were a young couple in love. Chasing each other on the hay bales and lots of giggles."

"Oh." That had to be embarrassing.

She nodded and rolled her eyes. "I contacted the girl privately and asked her not to trespass at my place anymore. Might seem extreme, but after being married to Rex, I take security seriously. I would never want to mistake someone for my ex."

"I understand. That could get someone shot." Chandler said nothing more, but he could tell Bristol's life had been ruled by her marriage to Rex. Even when he went to prison, she'd never been free of him. And no matter the measures she'd taken to be careful, her son had still been abducted. "Let's check out your barn."

"I'm okay doing it by myself. I do it every day. Even Spencer is used to our routine. It's a part of our life."

"Let me help anyway." Chandler found it sad the boy couldn't be a normal kid. He didn't know if the boy understood, but one day he would. Of course, now Spencer would probably have memories of the kidnapping, even if he did come home soon. What kind of damage would that do to him?

Bristol motioned for Chandler to follow her out the back door. She relocked it before heading toward the red barn. Wind blew the grass, and crickets chirped. Somewhere frogs croaked, telling him there was probably a pond nearby. The bloodhound roamed between them. "Tucker seems to be taken with you. Have you thought of getting a dog for protection?"

"I have. But I work during the day and have been taking classes at night. I can barely keep up with Spencer and my homework. A dog needs to be walked and played with. It's just not fair to one."

As much as he hated to admit it, she was probably right. It took time to tend to a dog's needs, and Bristol had her hands full. So much responsibility. The well-traveled path to the barn wasn't lit, but Bristol carried a powerful flashlight.

She wiggled the door handle, and then a concerned expression crossed her face. She wiggled it again. No sound. "Get back."

"What's wrong?"

She continued to step away from the structure, and the .45 appeared in her hand. She whispered, "The bell didn't ring."

Chandler grabbed Tucker's harness. "Stay." He turned to her. "Go take cover. I'll check out the barn."

"No. This is my life someone is wreaking havoc on. I'm staying."

"Is there anything valuable inside? Something someone needed? Is this what Spencer's abduction is about?"

"I don't know. If I knew I had something in my care, I'd turn it over. I just want my son back."

Instead of returning to the house, Bristol moved beside him, both of them with their weapons drawn.

He was going to open the door, but he wished Bristol was not in the line of danger. Out of town, out of harm's way. After he checked the barn, he was going to convince her to get to safety. His hand grabbed the handle and yanked the door open.

TWELVE

Bristol held her gun ready and prepared herself for the worst as the door swung wide.

No gunfire or explosions.

Chandler waited a few seconds before he stepped into the opening.

She pointed the light into the rafters and along the back wall. Several tools lay scattered on the ground, and some were on shelves or hung from hooks. A saddle sat on the saddle tree.

He whispered, "I'm going in. I'd rather you stay here so you can flee if need be."

She didn't mess with answering but shone the light ahead of his steps so he could see where he was going. She remained a few feet behind him but stayed with him and the dog. Her gaze searched the structure, trying to figure out what someone had been doing in here. She turned and saw the bell lying in the hay. Had the wind shaken the door and knocked it off? It had happened once or twice before, but only when it was extremely gusty. There had not been more than a slight breeze the last two days.

He glanced over to the stalls while Tucker sniffed the

ground. Chandler dropped his gun to his side. "Nothing. If someone was out here, they're gone."

"What about the loft?"

He glanced up. "Let me check it out."

The upper level was narrow and looked to be overflowing with years of stuff stored. It didn't take him a minute to look. He climbed back down the ladder. "Clear."

"We've got to be missing something. Someone was here." To be double sure, she walked around the barn, taking her time and pointing her light at everything. She didn't want to miss anything that had been removed or put inside.

"You said the place belongs to the lady in the nursing home—Mrs...."

"Graham. Edna Graham."

"Is it possible someone had permission to be in the barn and came by? Like, does Mrs. Graham have any kids, or the guy who leases the pasture?"

"Her two kids live down south near the Gulf and are not in great health. They've never been by. And the guy who leases the pasture is a neighbor and has his own tools. I suppose he could've dropped by, but I don't buy that since he never comes by without calling to let me know first."

She aimed the flashlight into the stall, and a mouse scurried out from old hay, making her jump. "Stupid mouse scared me to death."

Chandler waited patiently by the door and gazed out. "Do you see anything?"

"No. But I trust your judgment. If you think someone was here, then I must assume they were. The big question is why."

The admission that he trusted her judgment pleased

her. Aside from when she and Rex had dated, her ex had always talked to her like a child. He'd laugh at her concerns and tell her she had nothing to "worry her pretty head about." To this day, the phrase grated on her nerves. What had Chandler asked? *Why.* "I can't think of one thing someone would be after."

"Maybe you have something you're not aware of, or someone believes you have something and intends to use Spencer as leverage."

"Could be… That has to be it. But why doesn't that person just tell me what they want? It'd be so much easier. How do they expect me to hand something over if I don't know what it is? And why take Spencer? My mind keeps returning to Rex."

"He's dead."

"I know. But surely he could've become friends with someone in prison and convinced them I have something of value. But what? To my knowledge, he didn't even know where I lived, especially since he went to prison soon after I left him."

"We need to check his phone records while he was in prison, concentrating on the last couple of months." Chandler locked the barn door after Bristol repositioned the bell on the handle. She wanted to ask him to drive her around and look for the suspect's truck. But that was almost certain to be a waste of time. It was unlikely the man was still driving it.

The rotting washstand Mrs. Graham used to plant flowers in stood along the outside of the barn wall. The flashlight glistened off something inside the porcelain bowl. She had made the trek around the barn every day for almost two years—anything out of place stuck out. She hurried over to it.

"What is it?"

Her eyes focused. A photo lay in the washbowl, weighted down by a rock. The picture showed two men huddled together in deep conversation—the man on the left was Rufus Lance. She didn't recognize the older man on the right. A bag of what she presumed to be drugs was being passed from the older man to Rufus.

Chandler moved beside her. "Don't touch it."

She turned. "I wasn't going to. Looks like a photo of Rufus Lance, an old friend of Rex, making a drug deal. This is Lance, but who is the older guy?"

She continued to stare while moving the flashlight for a better view.

Using the tail of his shirt, Chandler snatched up the photo. He moved it closer, his forehead wrinkling. He placed it inside his shirt and headed toward the house.

"Hey, wait up. Do you recognize the other guy? Is this what someone wanted me to see?"

He kept walking. "I don't know why someone was in your barn or left the photo, presumably for you to find."

Something was wrong. Tension radiated off Chandler like an injured rabbit with buzzards circling. "Do you know the other man in the picture?"

"I don't want to talk about it."

"Chandler Murphy," she yelled. She ran in front of him, cutting him off and causing him to bump into her. "Who is the man in the picture?"

"Someone is trying to throw us off track. It's not real."

"What's not real? The photo?" She couldn't miss the pain in his eyes, but she had too much at stake to let this go. She lowered her voice. "Chandler, talk to me.

Who is the other guy? This could be the break we've been waiting for."

He looked up at the sky. "The man in the photo is my dad."

Chandler drew a breath, trying to calm his emotions, but it was no use. Confusion swirled as he tried to make sense of it. The man in the picture couldn't be his dad. Chandler strode toward his truck, needing to get away—to be alone and think.

Bristol kept his pace, practically running to keep up. "How do you know it's not him? The photo was probably taken several years ago."

"My dad didn't buy drugs. Now or then. He's dead." He slung open his truck door and climbed in. After Tucker jumped into the passenger seat, Chandler shut the door and rolled down the window.

"Probably not. Maybe it was a setup—a sting— whatever you call it."

"Dad worked undercover, but he didn't work stings like you suggest. If so, I would've known about it."

She cocked her head. "Why are you so upset? Is there something I'm missing?"

He removed the photo from his shirt with his shirt-tail, careful not to leave prints. He turned on the interior light and snapped a picture with his cell phone. After he'd enlarged it, he pointed the screen at her. "You notice anything?"

She took the cell phone from him. At first, she shook her head, but then she squinted. "Wait. That's Frilly's Fried Pickles on the square in downtown Liberty."

"The owner only bought it a year ago. There is no possible way my dad is alive. If he was, he would've come home." Simon wouldn't have let his family believe he were dead and put them through such misery. "Someone is trying to throw us off the trail."

"Where are you going?"

"To see someone who can look at this photo for evidence of it being manipulated. Get some sleep, and I'll call you in a bit."

Her eyes narrowed, and she released a deep sigh. "For what it's worth, I'm sorry."

He nodded, put the truck into Drive and took off. This case had just gotten more personal. Who'd planted the photo at Bristol's place? Was someone trying to warn them? If Chandler continued to investigate, would he find something that would turn his world upside down?

He turned onto the road and noticed Bristol standing on her porch, watching him pull away. Was he capable of helping her, or was everything going to come tumbling down?

If the photo had been meant to distract him, it worked.

Concern for Bristol gnawed at him. He didn't think there was enough evidence to prove she should be in WITSEC, but he'd push for it if he thought she needed it. Their biggest obstacle was figuring out who had kidnapped Spencer and who was after her.

That and what the abduction had to do with his dad. Instead of getting to the truth, more loose ends emerged.

Maybe he should get Josie Hunt to watch Bristol. Josie had gone through the academy. She'd worked as an investigator with the police department and then had started volunteering with Bring the Children Home Project before the long hours with the police no longer worked with her schedule. Three years ago, Josie had struck out on her own as a private investigator. Being that she had been up late helping them, he'd give her a couple more hours' sleep before he called her.

First, he needed to know if the photo of his dad had been manipulated. It had to be. The best person he knew who was good at dealing with photography probably wouldn't want to help him. He was tempted to contact someone else, but he needed to be certain. As he drove into Liberty, he turned along the railroad tracks and then again onto a dark street. Liberty, for the most part, was quiet, with minor crime, but this side of town made the majority of the calls to law enforcement.

He pulled into the parking lot of the Park Villa Apartments, a sad collection of buildings. Plywood covered several windows where the glass had been broken out, and the cries of a baby sounded from one of the apartments. He quickly climbed the metal stairs to the second floor and knocked on the door.

He waited and then knocked again when he didn't hear movement. "Sydney? It's Chandler—open up."

Finally, a rustling from her apartment. The door swung open. A woman with wild hair had a pistol pointed at him. "What do ya want?"

"Sis, it's me. Chandler." He put his hands in the air.

Blue eyes blinked, but the gun remained aimed. "Why are you here?"

"Put the gun down. Please."

"Long time no see, brother." She hesitated and then dropped the gun to her side. "Come on in."

He followed her, and the first thing he noticed was that the room was clean and picked up. Old furniture still decorated the room, but brightly colored pillows and houseplants gave the place a welcoming feel—unlike the last time he'd visited. "I need a favor."

"A favor for you? You've got to be kidding."

"This is important."

She tilted her head and stared. "What is it?"

"I need you to look at this photo for me. Tell me if it's real or manipulated."

Her hands rested on her hips as her eyes narrowed. "This must be important. But why me? Surely there are people in your department that can give you the same information."

He held out the photo. "Because of this."

His sister took the evidence bag and glanced at the photo, and then her gaze went back to him. "Where did you find this? The pickle place is new."

"I know." He debated whether to tell her what was going on with Rex Edwards, but it was Sydney's right to know as much as his. He explained about Bristol's missing son and all that had transpired.

She stared at the photo, and sadness settled into her expression. "Okay. I'll do it. Might take me a bit. I can say from first glance, the picture looks untouched. I'll call you as soon as I know something."

"Thanks."

She followed him to the door. "I hope it is him. I know you've been trying to solve his case for a long time."

"You look good, sis."

Her gaze narrowed, and she dipped her head to one side, scrutinizing him.

He could feel her watching him as he headed down the stairs. It was good to see her again. Maybe her life was coming together.

Thirty minutes later, instead of going home to bed, he arrived at the station. He put on a fresh pot of coffee and fired up his laptop. As much as he wanted to know if the photo was real, he'd wait to hear back from Sydney before going down that trail. Whoever had left it intended to distract him, which meant he and Bristol were on the right track.

Once he had a brewed mug, he opened Rex Edwards's old files and paid particular attention to the man's friends. Chandler opened a blank document on his computer and inserted a table to make it easy to put the connections into separate categories. The major difference in the new graph was the contacts from those who were in prison or were free but whom Rex had communicated with. He also created a separate category for the people Rex hadn't seen since before prison. He rearranged the list in order of priority, starting with Rufus Lance. You never knew who were linked to others and how careful Rex had been to cover his tracks. Like Bristol, he believed whoever had Spencer was connected to her ex.

Two hours later, Chandler closed his laptop and rolled his neck, trying to loosen his muscles. A couple of names reappeared multiple times, and he saved their information on his phone. He'd check those out first.

After filling a tumbler with coffee, he returned to his desk and got busy filling out the paperwork from last night's events. If a warrant was required for a search, it was easier if all the paperwork was already in order.

He'd no sooner finished filling in the last bit of information than Sheriff Carroll strode up to his desk. "What did you get?"

Chandler was used to the sheriff's gruff ways. His boss didn't feel the need to waste time on chitchat, for which he was thankful. Except for the photo of his dad found outside Bristol's barn, he filled the sheriff in on what had happened last night.

His boss looked thoughtful. "We need to get Bristol Delaney more protection. I'll assign Deputy Perkins to watch over her."

The sheriff rarely suggested someone need protection. Since it was possible whoever had attacked him and Bristol was long gone, it surprised Chandler his boss had made the offer. Hattie Perkins was a good deputy, but she had four kids at home who were involved in baseball and track. He'd heard her complain lately about the overtime the deputies were getting. Josie wasn't married and didn't have children, so having her watch Bristol twenty-four hours straight seemed to be more logical. "That sounds great…"

"But…?" Carroll's eyebrows shot up in question.

"Deputy Perkins has vacation next week and has been busy with her kids' sports lately."

"Are you saying you think Perkins wouldn't do the job?"

Chandler was quick to answer. "Never. It's well-known Perkins is an excellent deputy, but I'd hate for her to be on babysitting duty." He hated the term *babysitting duty*, but it was commonly used, especially when an officer didn't want to do it. "I was thinking of Josie Hunt with Bring the Children Home Project."

The sheriff nodded. "Hunt is good, and there should be enough in the budget for a couple of days. Hunt would keep Hattie free for her normal duties. Have you already asked her?" He pinned him with a stare.

"Not until I talked to you."

"Smart thinking, Murphy. Keep me updated where Delaney is staying." The sheriff walked away.

The sheriff offering to give Bristol protection nagged at the back of his mind. It was probably because Chandler was close to the case. Sheriff Carroll was tough on the exterior and rarely showed his caring heart to the people who worked for him. Several months ago, a deputy had voiced safety concerns regarding a witness to a shooting that killed a sixty-three-year-old convenience store clerk, but the sheriff had turned it down due to staff shortages. A day later, that witness had ended up in the hospital, beaten, with three broken ribs and a fractured jaw. Maybe the sheriff had learned his lesson.

He guessed Josie would be awake, so he called her.

"Hey, Chandler. You need another ride?"

"No." He smiled, knowing she was teasing. "I'm concerned for Bristol. I want to check out some leads today but would rather not have to keep an eye on her. Would you be able to stay with her?"

"She's not home."

"What do you mean? I just dropped her off a couple of hours ago."

"She called about thirty minutes ago to ask what I had learned about Rex's friends—in particular, Rufus Lance. Lance moved to Missouri a year ago, but I gave her a couple of names. Hope that was okay."

His jaw clenched. "Which ones?"

"Hold on." There was shuffling in the background. "Uh, they like to be known as Flack and Tito, but their arrest records say Michael McMillan and Derek White."

There were several brothers and cousins in the McMillan family who couldn't stay out of trouble. Mainly petty stuff, but a couple of them were into more violent crime. He didn't recall Flack. "Did you give Bristol their information?"

"Just their workplace—the muffler shop on Main Street. Tito's information was over two years old—a home address on the south side of town—but I can send the addresses to you."

"Yeah. Send me whatever you sent her."

"And hey—" Josie hurried to get the words in.

"Yeah?"

"I hope she doesn't get into trouble. I offered to go with her, but she said she was driving by the locations and had no intention of stopping. She promised to let me know if she found anything. I'll check out one of the places if you want."

He wanted to tell Josie he could handle it but reconsidered. As much as he hated to ask for help, he swallowed his pride. "I would appreciate that. I'll check out the muffler shop. Thanks." After he clicked off, he hurried to his borrowed truck. He glanced down at the text Josie had sent and put the address to the muffler shop into his GPS. Technically it was the Liberty Police's jurisdiction, but he didn't plan on seeking a suspect. He just wanted to check on Bristol.

Chandler had also learned Lance moved to another state, which had him questioning the photo.

With a quick punch of the button on his cell phone, he hit Bristol's number. No answer.

He didn't blame Josie, but he wished she hadn't given her the information. Bristol carried a pistol, but her emotions were running high.

A few minutes later, he pulled into Big Daddy's Mufflers and Brakes and parked in front of an Oldsmobile that was about to exit that bay.

"Hey!" A man in a greasy shirt came out waving his arms. "You need to move your vehicle."

Chandler stepped out of his unmarked pickup, and the guy's gaze instantly went to the badge on his belt.

"I didn't do nothin'." The long-haired guy glanced back at the office.

Chandler couldn't see through the grimy windows, but he heard a long squeak like a chair skidded across tile. "Is Mike McMillan here?"

"Don't know who you're talking about." The worker's head bobbed nervously.

"Flack?"

The guy glanced around like he was going to take off, but Chandler whistled for Tucker. His canine was only trained to rescue, but this man didn't know that. Tucker leaped from the front seat and trotted their way.

Chandler said, "I wouldn't move if I were you, Flack."

The man held his hands out to Tucker and bounced from one foot to the other.

Tucker's ears went up, and he barked.

"Where have you been the last couple of nights?" Chandler crossed his arms over his chest.

"Nowhere," Flack shouted as he kept his attention on Tucker.

Movement in the shop caught Chandler's eye. A large older man dressed in coveralls stood in the doorway with a half-smoked cigar shoved between his lips.

Chandler could only guess this was Big Daddy. Even though Tucker was harmless, he grabbed his harness and pulled it tight like he was having to restrain him.

Flack continued to spout, "I didn't take nothing. That was Tito and the rest of 'em."

"Shut up, man! I'm gonna pound you if you say another word." A thirtysomething man dressed in running shoes emerged from the shadows. A tight tank top revealed a wide chest and bulging biceps. His dark eyes met Chandler's. "We don't have anything to say to you."

The loud shouts made Tucker bark again.

"Call your dog off, man," Flack begged.

"Answer a couple of questions, and I may leave you alone." For good measure, he widened his stance like he could barely contain the hound and hoped Tucker's wagging tail didn't give his game away.

"What is it?"

"Tell me about Rex Edwards."

"Edwards," both men said in unison.

Tito lifted his chin. "What do you want with Edwards?"

Chandler answered, "Tell me what you know about his son."

"His son?" Flack's voice came out high-pitched. "I didn't know he had a kid."

Tito slapped Flack in the chest. "Keep your mouth shut, dude." The big guy turned his attention back to Chandler. "We don't keep up with Edwards's offspring. As far as I know, he had kids spread all over this state. Ain't none of my business."

Chandler got the feeling they knew nothing about the kidnapping. "What about his ex-wife?"

"I only seen the broad a couple of times." Tito grinned, showing silver caps on his front teeth. "A real boring piece of work, but pretty to look at."

"Don't suppose you've seen her the last couple of days?"

Tito shook his head. "Nah. But I don't know why all the questions. I heard Rexy boy got himself offed in prison."

Chandler glanced back to Flack. "Have you seen her?"

"No." He shrugged. "Never met her."

"Do me a favor. If you see Rex's son or hear anything, let me know." He held out his card to Flack, who snatched it while eyeing the dog.

"What's in it for me?"

Chandler smiled. "Let's say I won't spend my time

uncovering what you've been stealing this past week-
end." Careful not to turn his back on them, he took
Tucker by the leash and got back in his truck. Flack
visibly relaxed, but Tito watched him until he pulled
out of the place.

Those two were dirty, but he believed them when
they said they hadn't heard of Rex's son or seen Bristol.
Well, he believed Flack, anyway. Tito was a dangerous
character. If Bristol wasn't here, she must've gone to
the other address.

He tried calling her again, and when she didn't answer, he dialed Josie.

"This is Josie."

"Have you heard from Bristol?"

"Sorry, not yet. But I should be at Tito's place in five
minutes. I'll let you know if she's there."

"Okay." He cleared his throat so his tone didn't come
out sharp. "I'll be there in ten."

After he disconnected, he attempted to shove concern aside, but worry settled like a baseball in his gut.
There was no way to keep her safe if she ran off on her
own. He gritted his teeth. "Where are you, Bristol?"

THIRTEEN

The old Chevy's shocks were shot, and the driver's seat had a large rip in it, but Bristol didn't care. Mrs. Graham had told her more than once if she ever needed to borrow the truck to take it. She'd never needed it until now. Outside town, she had filled up with gas. If she was going to look for the maroon truck, or whatever the suspect was driving now, she didn't want to have to stop later. Hopefully, Tito would be the guy driving it, and Spencer might even be at the house.

The morning sun shone through the dirty windshield, the glare blinding her. She hit the brakes and pulled to the side of the paved road. She wasn't familiar with the area, but at least she wasn't worried about someone recognizing her vehicle.

She took off again until she came to a sharp curve in the road. On the other side, three run-down houses sat in a row. Two were single-wide mobile homes, and the last one was an old wooden house without a speck of paint. Several vehicles sat in each of the yards, one on blocks. But none of them looked like the ones that had been involved in the chase. Disappointment fell on her.

Five or six dogs jumped off the dilapidated porch and rushed to her car, barking in a chaotic frenzy.

So much for quietly driving by so as to not draw attention to herself. The dogs continued to chase her truck for a quarter of a mile before they gave up and headed back toward their home. A check in her rearview mirror showed no other vehicle in pursuit.

The paved road came to a dead end about a mile later. A small path led into a pasture, but she didn't think it was a public road. With no other alternative, she turned the truck around. Dread filled her as she came to the houses again, hoping the dogs didn't return. She glanced toward the frame house and did a double take. A newer-model red Dodge Charger convertible sat in the drive that hadn't been there a few minutes ago. It was out of place among the junkers.

A man in a baseball cap stood at the house door, but she couldn't make out his features at this distance. She glanced back to the road and let out a squeal. A Ford Bronco was right in front of her.

She jerked the wheel to her right and slammed on her brakes.

The commotion brought the dogs again and another barking tirade.

The driver's window of the Bronco rolled down, and Josie Hunt stared back at her.

"I'm so sorry. I was looking at the vehicles in the yard."

Josie glanced back toward the houses. "I came to make certain you were all right. Chandler has been trying to get ahold of you."

"What? Oh." Bristol grabbed her cell phone from her purse. "I must've accidentally turned it on silent. It's a new phone."

Josie looked again at the houses. "Did you learn anything?"

"No." She looked in the same direction. The man in the cap was no longer in sight. "I don't recognize any of these cars as the ones that chased us. But that convertible just showed up."

"Okay. Let's get out of the road. Do you know where the Corner Diner is?"

"Yeah."

"Okay. Let's meet there. We need to talk."

As Bristol drove away, she was glad to have Josie to talk to. She'd never lived in the same place long enough to make friends—not long-lasting ones, anyway. As she got older, she felt it was a waste of time to even try. Friendly acquaintances were how she viewed them. Someone to smile and say hello to, but she didn't hold her breath for a relationship. She'd never been able to depend on anyone before, and it was easier to keep things simple. Just her and Spencer.

She swallowed.

Spencer was gone. She had to get her boy back.

Chandler has been trying to get ahold of you. Josie's words flowed back to her. Did he have news? Had he learned something that could lead her to Spencer? She punched in his number on her phone.

"Where are you?"

The irritation in his voice radiated loud and clear, but she kept calm. "I turned the volume down on my phone. Sorry."

He let out a growl. "I've been trying to find you. I thought someone had attacked you again."

Her heart picked up the pace, but she drew a deep breath. "I said I was sorry. I can see where that might make you worry."

"Worry? Bristol, someone tried to kill us. I was

scared to death." Silence. When he spoke again, his voice had dropped a notch. "Did you learn anything?"

"Not really. I was hoping to find the maroon truck. Nothing but several old cars and one convertible." His reaction still irked her. She reminded herself it did little good to argue, but... "How can you expect me to sit back and do nothing? I will not be told what to do."

A few seconds of silence. "I was concerned for your safety. Let me know your plans next time. Please."

She blinked at the phone, surprised he didn't berate her or talk down to her. He was concerned. "Okay. I'm meeting Josie at the Corner Diner."

"I'll see you there."

After he clicked off, she stared at the phone. She didn't owe him an explanation. Did she? She just wanted to find her son, and the deputy was a means to an end. As soon as the thought entered her mind, shame niggled at her conscious. Her mom had dragged her from one relationship to another like Bristol held no importance and was just along for the ride. She never wanted to treat anyone like that. Especially someone like Chandler, who was trying to protect her.

After she found Spencer, what then?

Following her graduation after the summer session, she'd find a new place to live where no one knew her. Start over. Again. But this time, the thought of being in a strange town with no acquaintances sounded depressing.

And why did Chandler flit through her mind?

When Chandler got out of his truck at the diner, Josie's Bronco was pulling in, and an older pickup truck followed behind her. Bristol got out of the truck and squared her shoulders.

He folded his arms across his chest as his gaze met hers. Even though he guessed she wanted to look away, she didn't. Not even a blink.

A door slammed. "I'm glad you joined us."

Chandler shot Josie a smile.

Josie glanced from Bristol to Chandler. It sounded like she mumbled, "Awkward." Then she proceeded to the door.

He held the door while they filed in.

Windows surrounded the place, letting in the sunlight. Booths lined the walls, and tables filled the center of the room. Josie picked the circular booth in the back corner and slid in first. Chandler waited for Bristol to sit, which left her in the middle.

He turned to Bristol. "Did you learn anything?"

She shook her head and explained about the multiple cars, the dogs chasing her and meeting Josie.

"You didn't see anyone?" Chandler raised an eyebrow.

"Wait. Yes, I did." She waited while a waitress gave each of them a glass of water and took their drink orders. After the young lady walked away, Bristol continued, "There was a big guy in a baseball cap on the porch. He was driving a convertible. By the time I almost hit Josie, he was gone." She shrugged. "I'm guessing he went inside."

"What kind of convertible?"

"It was red and looked like a Dodge Charger. Anyone you know drive that?"

He thought for a second. "I've seen a few around, but nothing in particular."

"I don't know anyone who drives a Charger," Josie added.

Chandler said, "When we're through eating, I'll drive by the address and see if the car is still there."

Josie put her elbows on the table. "Have you heard from Bliss?"

"She's still in West Texas helping Annie Brenner with a case." Chandler wished she were here. She had a knack for solving missing-children's cases.

Bristol looked at Josie. "Who's Bliss and Annie?"

"Bliss Walker is an ex–US marshal who founded and owns the Bring the Children Home Project. Annie is the team's weapons instructor."

"Really? A US marshal?"

Josie nodded. "Her son disappeared eight or nine years ago, and after authorities couldn't find him, it motivated her to retire and start the program. She dedicates all her time trying to find missing children."

As he listened to the two women visit, he itched to get them back to discussing the case. But he didn't know where else to go with it. While at the station, he'd learned the helicopter was not being used today in Spencer's search due to mechanical issues. The local news and radio stations aired an interview with Sheriff Carroll about the kidnapping where he also provided the number for a tip hotline. A couple of deputies, along with several volunteers, were scouring the area, handing out flyers with contact information and Spencer's photo.

He found himself watching Bristol and her mannerisms. Her cheeks creased with dimples, giving her a sweet, attractive appearance. How could an intelligent lady like this wind up falling for someone as corrupt as Rex?

For the first time in a long time, he was attracted to someone.

Suddenly, she turned to him. "What made you want to join the Bring the Children Home Project?"

Chandler glanced away. How did one explain how he caused his family's trouble? Would Bristol be able to trust him or look him in the eyes again? And he'd never discussed his reasons with Josie, either. He went for the simple answer. "It's a much-needed program. Sometimes authorities can use assistance with finding kids, and I wanted to be a part of it."

The truth was, Chandler's younger sister, Sydney, ran away from home when she was fifteen. She was two years younger than himself. During her freshman year in high school, it irritated her that their parents wanted her to get a part-time job in the summer instead of spending most of her time with her boyfriend. He hung out at a local pool hall mainly playing video games, which her parents didn't like. One day, Sydney told their parents she was going to the mall with friends but didn't return home that afternoon. Thinking she was just late, their parents were more angry than scared.

Until later that night, when by nine thirty, Sydney still wasn't home.

After several phone calls, his parents learned she had been seen with her boyfriend on the outskirts of town. The police were called, but law enforcement figured she'd be coming back home and didn't act until forty-eight hours later. They never formed a search party or actively looked but made a few phone calls and contacted the boy's parents. When the boyfriend showed up the following week, alone, the police finally made inquiries. Almost three weeks later, a Dallas woman found Sydney on the south side of the city in an alley. His sister spent ten days in the ICU recovering from a drug overdose and never fully got off the bad road. As soon as she was able, Sydney was gone again. A life of drugs and homeless shelters—if she was lucky. If not, she lived in abandoned buildings or stayed with anyone who'd give her a place to sleep.

After his sister's decline, Chandler's dad had come down hard on him, telling him to take life more seriously. Chandler had always felt his parents—or maybe just his dad—blamed Chandler for his sister's problems, like she'd followed in his footsteps.

He'd resented it at the time, although looking back, he knew they were right in some ways. Not drugs. But Chandler liked to do his thing and enjoyed life. It was after he joined the sheriff's department when he witnessed other teens who had gone missing and the department's slow response that he started volunteering with the Bring the Children Home Project. Authorities were eager to find young children who they believed were taken against their will. But when a teen ran away and didn't want to be found, it could be a frustrating cycle that had no end—sometimes eliciting law agencies to wait to see if the child came home on their own.

Bristol watched him, and he wished she'd quit staring. It was like she could tell he wasn't telling her the whole truth.

"I'm glad you're on the team—whatever your reasons. I can't imagine what it's like for parents who never find their child."

"Me, too," Josie said with a faraway look in her eyes.

The waitress brought their food, and he was glad for the distraction. He kept trying to decide whether he wanted Bristol with him so he could keep an eye on her or if he should suggest she go with Josie. His team member was capable of doing her job, but he didn't like the thought of Bristol being out of his sight.

He didn't intend to get in a romantic relationship until his father's case was solved and had stuck to his guns without reservation. Only now did he see that as a problem.

FOURTEEN

Bristol was surprised Chandler asked her to go with him after they left the diner. She supposed it worked well, because Josie said she was pursuing something for the case. Bristol and Chandler had gone back to the sheriff's department, where he talked to officers while she napped in a chair beside his desk.

By midafternoon with no other leads, they relieved the other deputies who were passing out flyers and knocking on doors. Most residents had heard about the kidnapping and were keeping an eye out for the maroon truck. It was a long and frustrating process, but it was better than waiting at home for the phone to ring.

As the sun went down, they finally had to call it quits and the other volunteers went home to eat supper and to be with their families.

Bristol stared out the passenger window as the nighttime scenery whizzed past. Chandler had been quiet ever since they'd gotten in the truck and was probably just as disgruntled as she. The massive headache pushing at her temples was not helping, nor her aching feet. Her throat tightened while she tried not to think about how she'd failed her son.

Where was he?

A whimper came from the back seat and then warmth landed on her shoulder. She patted Tucker's head, savoring the softness of his fur and glad for the comfort. How did dogs sense when you needed them the most? Tucker had stayed with them all afternoon while scouring the neighborhoods. Adults and kids alike had taken to the sweet bloodhound.

When they passed the turn to her house, she glanced at Chandler. "Where are we going?"

"To my parents' house."

She swallowed down the sudden dryness in her throat. "Why?"

"You're going to get some sleep while I go through some of my dad's things."

Irritation clawed at her even though she knew he was trying to help—the subject of his dad was a sensitive one. "I took a nap and should be good for a while."

He exhaled a deep breath. "I'm tired, Bristol. Neither of us has had much sleep. I want to catch this guy, but I keep coming back to my dad. First, Anthony mentioned him at the prison, and then the photo of him was left at your place. There must be a connection between my dad and Rex or Lance. Something was going on that I didn't know about."

"I can help you. I'm certain you've looked through his things before."

"I have. But this is something I must do."

"Don't give me the 'something I must do' excuse. I've had to turn over my whole life to you. Certainly, I can go through some of your life." Suddenly, a thought came to her. Maybe Chandler was afraid his dad had been into something criminal. Like possibly his dad was guilty of something and he didn't want anyone else to find out. No way. From the little bit she'd learned,

Simon Murphy was one of the good guys. Even so, the photo suggested he had been buying drugs. After being set up by Rex, she'd never assume someone's guilt. "Is there a reason you don't want my help? Something to do with that photo of your dad?"

He frowned. "I just thought you needed rest."

"Have you heard back on if the photograph was real or not?"

He continued to look straight ahead. "Not yet."

She laid her head against the seat and stared out the window. "I'm running on fumes, but I don't think I could sleep."

"Fair enough."

The case kept going through her mind, but no new ideas came to her. The main thought that kept returning was when Rex had used her to smuggle drugs in her coat. Did he tell others she'd helped him? Did some dealer or user believe she was involved in and had access to narcotics?

The thought terrified her.

Chandler turned on the paved rural road, and the trees whizzed by her window. His mom's place was out in the country among other farms and ranches. He pulled down the long drive that snaked around a small lake to the back of the property. Brahman cattle lay in the grass under the moonlight. The two-story white home with a wraparound porch stood out against the dark horizon. Her heart constricted as the truck rolled to a stop.

Maybe she should lie down somewhere if it'd keep her from talking to his family. She didn't think she could handle any more right now.

"We're here." He shot her a quick glance. "You all right?"

Was her tension that obvious? "Sure." Sarcasm laced her tone. "Why wouldn't I be?"

His hazel eyes connected with hers under the security light. "My mom is nice."

"I guessed that." She needed to get ahold of herself. Snapping only made her seem more vulnerable. Why was it when she met nice families it rubbed her the wrong way? She prayed often to let go of jealousy. Even though many families appeared perfect, she knew no one was without struggles, and why be bothered by happy families when that was what she aspired for her and Spencer?

"Let's go in."

She followed him and Tucker up the sidewalk and waited for him to open the front door. The light in the entryway was the only one on in the house.

"Mom is probably in bed, and she sleeps soundly."

"I'm awake." An older woman with gray highlights and medium-length hair appeared in the door. The cotton pajama bottoms and soft shirt looked classy on her. Bright green eyes went to Bristol.

"Didn't mean to drop by so late, Mom. You don't mind, do you?"

"Of course not." She waved her hand. "Come on in."

Bristol followed Chandler into a spacious foyer with a wooden floor and tall ceilings.

"This is Bristol, who I told you about—" he pointed to her " —and this is my mom."

Bristol smiled, even though she would like to know what Chandler had said about her. "Glad to meet you, Mrs. Murphy."

"Please, call me Trudy. I'm not that formal. It's good to meet you, although I'm sorry about the circumstances. I'm going to leave you two alone, but if you need anything—

something to eat, or just someone to talk to—I'm here."
She glanced at the dog. "Tucker, you want to come with
me? Your doggy bed is waiting for you, and I have treats."

The bloodhound wagged his tail and followed her
out of the room.

"Thanks," Bristol called after her. Awkwardness hung
in the air as she forced herself not to look at Chandler.
His mom's friendliness seemed to mock Bristol, making
her feel second-class. But why? His mom was nothing
but friendly. Or was that the problem?

Had Bristol thought it was smart to get away from
her mom and hook up with Rex Edwards? Rex hadn't
had much of a family life. Was that one of the things
she'd found attractive about him? Bristol felt like she
could relate to Rex because he had no family to become a part of?

And with Chandler, the closeness he'd shared with
his relatives made her feel like an outcast. She'd felt on
even ground with Rex.

"You can lie down in Sydney's old room if you change
your mind."

"No, thanks. I couldn't sleep." She looked at him
then. "Tell me about your sister."

"I don't want to."

His honest forthrightness surprised her. "Why not?"

"You asked earlier why I started volunteering with
Bring the Children Home Project."

"Yeah." She sucked in a breath. "Did your sister go
missing?"

Circles formed under his eyes, and his hair stuck up
from him running his hand through it. "Temporarily as
a teenager, yeah, but authorities dragged their feet looking for her. They assumed she'd run away and would
return in a few days. We found her two weeks later, but

a lot of damage had already been done. I didn't want to see that happen with other families. I'd rather not talk about Sydney, but would prefer to help you. Come on." He motioned for her to follow. As she stared at his retreating back, she realized there was more to the deputy than she'd first thought. And sadly, his family had problems, too.

When she stepped into the room, she could feel the presence of Chandler's dad, even though she had never met him. A wooden desk sat against the wall and—except for a few hunting magazines, a mini laptop and a lamp—the room was spotless, free of clutter. A framed photo of Simon and Trudy sat on the desk, and another one with him and the whole family at the lake hung on the wall.

No one knew what had happened to the detective, but most assumed he had been murdered or he would've come home. Bristol wondered.

"Have a seat." Chandler pointed to the plush chair, and he grabbed a metal folding chair from the closet. He pulled it next to the desk and turned on the laptop.

"What was your dad working on at the time of his disappearance?" At his look, she hurried to continue. "I know he was looking into my ex-husband's activities. But anything in particular?"

He shook his head. "Dad was supposed to be investigating Rex's drug dealings. Connections to the higher-ups. Typical stuff, but dangerous."

"What makes you think there's a connection between your dad and Spencer's abduction and the attacks on me?"

His brows furrowed. "I don't know. Instinct more than anything. Dad was investigating Rex, and then he disappears. Rex got sent to jail, and right before he's supposed to be released, he gets killed and Spencer gets abducted. If another child had been taken from that daycare van, I'd think there wasn't a connection. But someone let the other children go and was only interested in Spencer."

"And the photo." At his stony glare, she continued, "You're not stating anything I haven't been thinking, like we're missing an important piece of the puzzle." She shoved the chair back, giving herself some room. "I keep wondering if the man who took my son believes he has something."

"But what could the boy have? He couldn't have witnessed something, right?" Chandler cocked his head at her.

"No way. Like what? He's either with me or at the daycare. And if he witnessed a crime, I doubt he'd be able to recall the details, anyway."

"That's what I was thinking, too. Okay, time to get busy. I'll check his laptop again." The computer powered up, and he entered a password that was scribbled on a sticky note.

"Your dad kept his password right there for anyone to find?"

He didn't even look up. "This was stuck here by the forensics team. After his disappearance, they searched his files for clues, but since it was his personal computer, we got it back when it was cleared."

"Makes sense."

He didn't mention the files in the book that sat beside the desk, but she wanted to help. Needed to do something. She withdrew a couple of files and riffled through them. Chandler glanced at her but said nothing.

Most were handwritten notes jotted down on paper. The dates indicated these were from six years ago, just one year before Simon disappeared. There were no names, just initials and locations. Sometimes the make and model of a vehicle.

After she searched through multiple files, a pattern developed. Dates, initials, locations and then a one- or two-word conclusion—like *drugs passed*, *no meeting*, *residence*. Sometimes photos followed. At first glance, she'd thought the detective had been disorganized in his notes, but the more she read, the more her appreciation grew.

Bristol assumed official reports were stored at the station and weren't allowed to be kept in a private residence, but it wouldn't hurt to ask. "Do you have copies of the official files your dad turned over to the police?"

"Huh?" He glanced up from the screen. After she repeated the question, he said, "No. I looked through them right after he disappeared, but I had to do it at the station."

"Okay." She stared at him as concern crossed his face. "Is something wrong?"

"Everything is fine." He didn't look up.

She smiled and held her palms in the air. "Seriously?"

He looked up at her. "There's nothing on his laptop for two weeks preceding his disappearance."

"Maybe you overlooked it." She got up and peeked over his shoulder as he scrolled down the dates. That was odd. "Were they there before?"

"I think so." He rubbed the back of his neck. "Right after we got the laptop back, I went through it and searched specifically for Rex Edwards. I remember thinking that my dad preferred handwritten notes instead of the computer. I always believed it was because he was used to the old-fashioned way."

"That makes sense. Let me see if there're notes from

that time period." She moved back to the documents and flipped through the papers. "You're right. There's nothing here. Is there any other place your dad kept his findings?"

"Not that I know of, but let me think."

"What about in his car?"

"That would be too obvious, and his vehicle was meticulously gone over by investigators." Chandler got to his feet and paced the floor. "How did I miss this before?"

"You'd just lost your dad and were trying to solve the case. Don't blame yourself."

He looked at her, and his gaze connected with hers. His face morphed into a pensive expression.

"What is it?" Bristol held her breath. Chandler had been close to his dad, and she knew he blamed himself for not realizing his dad was in trouble. But something had just crossed his mind. She wished he'd talk to her.

If he was correct and there was a connection, her son's life might depend on it.

Something wasn't right. Had the police hidden his dad's notes? If so, why? Maybe his dad stumbled onto something he wasn't supposed to find. But Chandler had gone through all the evidence. Surely he hadn't overlooked them.

Sheriff Carroll.

The sheriff had overseen the investigation. Had he hidden evidence? Chandler swiped his hand through his hair. He didn't enjoy having these thoughts about someone in the department protecting his father's killer. Or was the killer in the department?

He didn't care what he had to do, but he intended

to find his dad's notes from the last weeks before his dad disappeared.

"Who is *MC*?"

Chandler took the file Bristol was reading from her hand. Sure enough, *"M"C* with a question mark next to it. No photo attached, and no date listed, which was odd. His mind quickly sorted through law enforcement from the county. First the sheriff's department, and then on to the officers he could remember from the police department. There was a Monte Morrison and a Mack Sanders, but neither of them had a last name that matched. He finally said, "I don't know."

She stared at him. "And why are there quotations around the *M*?"

"Dad used quotations several times in his notes. If I was to guess, I'd say it's an alias."

"Hmm."

"What?" He didn't like the way Bristol said it. Like it would be something he wouldn't cherish.

"Does the sheriff have a nickname?"

"I haven't heard him called it in years, but people used to call him Sheriff Buckee."

"Why Buckee?"

"When he was younger, he used to ride in the sheriff's posse, you know, the group of deputies who carry flags and ride in events like rodeos and parades…"

She nodded.

"Well, one time Carroll picked a spirited horse. I'm sure you can figure out what happened."

Her eyebrows arched. "Took him for a ride?"

"Right in the middle of a July Fourth parade. No one calls him Buckee anymore except a few of the old-timers—including my dad."

"Okay, we'll assume your dad wasn't referring to the

sheriff. Let's go through these notes one more time and see if anyone has the same initials."

They both went through the huge stack of notes, but neither found a match. Frustration bit at him, for this was the first clue he'd had in a couple of years of going through his dad's stuff. But it was Bristol who'd found it, not him.

His mom stepped in the door. "Are either of you hungry?"

Chandler was quick to answer. "I'm not."

"Me neither." Bristol shook her head, but then she stopped. "But I probably should eat something."

A smile tugged at his mom's lips. She walked out of the room and returned carrying a plate of homemade cinnamon rolls, the smell carrying to him before she entered the room.

"These look delicious." Bristol tore the bread from the plate.

His mom brought in two glasses of milk.

"I was much hungrier than I realized." Bristol licked her fingers.

"Okay. I'd hate for these to go to waste." Chandler grabbed two large rolls. "Thanks, Mom. These are still hot."

Satisfaction lit his mother's lips. "Glad you changed your mind. Let me know if you need anything else."

"I will," he mumbled. The sweet pastry melted in his mouth, and stickiness covered his fingers. Lacking a napkin, he had no alternative but to lick the icing from his fingers. His mom was already out the door when he called her back.

She returned. "Yes?"

"Do you know anyone with the initials *MC*?"

"Hmm." Her mouth quirked as she thought. "No, not that I can recall. Is it important?"

"Maybe. You know how Dad always wrote his notes cryptically and used initials? A few days before he disappeared, he jotted down *MC* with a question mark. No photos or other info."

His mom's forehead wrinkled as she shook her head. "I can't think of anyone, but give me a little time to consider it."

"Okay. Thanks."

After she left the room, Bristol said, "I like her."

He glanced at her. "She's nice."

"She's more than that. Your mom cares a lot about her family, about you. You're blessed to have her."

Bristol's comments surprised him. Leslie Holmes, the lady he had been dating when his dad disappeared, had considered his family a distraction. She'd even complained that his mom was too involved and wanted him to become a mama's boy. Chandler had thought little about it at the time, but the comments made him pull away a bit, trying to prove he stood on his own two feet. Looking back, Leslie had been manipulative, but he'd been too blind to see it.

He gave Bristol another look. He didn't know much about her family. "What about your mom?"

She tensed. "What about her?"

"How was your relationship with her?"

Lines creased her forehead. "Fine. She tried to take care of me, but her biggest hurdle was bad romantic relationships. Did you find anything else during the week of your dad's disappearance?"

"Not yet." The abrupt change in subject didn't go unnoticed, but he could ask more questions later. He got back to work on the computer, but nothing presented itself. It seemed like Bristol was having progress with the handwritten notes. Was there more? Had his dad been worried about the case and put his papers somewhere else? Chandler got to his feet and went into the kitchen.

His mom looked up.

"Is there anywhere else Dad would've put his notes? I know it's a long shot, but I feel like we're missing something."

"The police already went through his car, but you can look again. It's sitting under the carport."

Bristol walked up behind him.

"I figure if there's anything in the vehicle, they would've found it. Was there a secret place he kept things? The garage or in his closet?"

"Not that I'm aware. I've gone through his things several times over the past few years."

He kept his tone even so as not to show his frustration. "Okay. Thanks anyway."

Bristol jerked her head toward the office, indicating he should follow.

"What is it?" He strode into the room.

"Your dad was a religious man."

"Sure, he was. My dad was quietly active."

She nodded. "I may've found something."

He tried to tap down hope in case it didn't pan out. "Show me."

She reached for his dad's Bible and then opened it. "Right here. There are notes on a sermon dated three weeks before his disappearance."

"He often wrote down the Scriptures and would look at them later."

"Here's the initials *'M'C* again."

Chandler glanced over her shoulder.

Matthew 23:25. *"M"C.*

"Does *MC* have something to do with the Bible?"

"I don't think so." Chandler took the Bible and quickly looked up the verse and read it out loud.

"Woe unto you, scribes and Pharisees, hypocrites! for ye make clean the outside of the cup and of the platter, but within they are full of extortion and excess."

Bristol whistled. "Sounds like a person who everyone believes is a good guy but isn't."

"Yeah." Chandler wondered if this *"M"C* went to worship services. He hurried to find his mom. "Do you have a directory of the church?"

"Uh, yeah. Hold on." She dug in the kitchen drawer and pulled out a small white book. "Here it is. A lot of young people use the online directory, but I still find this more convenient."

"Thanks," he mumbled and strode back into the office. "I have the church directory."

Bristol looked over her shoulder as he skimmed the names. "Go straight to the *C*s."

Their congregation wasn't large, but he did as she suggested. "Last names are Carroll, Carver, Clay, Cole and Crabtree."

Bristol pointed. "Marianne Carroll is the only person with the correct initials."

"The sheriff's wife?" A woman who'd been kind to Chandler since he was a child.

His mom whisked into the room. "What about Marianne?"

Chandler laid the directory on the desk and grabbed his dad's Bible. He held it out with the page open to his mom. "We were trying to find the person who Dad was talking about."

His mom's mouth dropped open. "Marianne is one of the sweetest women I know. She's always tending to the sick and elderly. Your father would've told me if he suspected her, and just because he jotted the note in his Bible doesn't mean the person went to services with us."

"You're right." He didn't want to contradict his mom, but his dad had been referring to someone everyone believed was nice and did good deeds. Chandler wanted to dismiss the thought as ludicrous, but he simply didn't know. If it wasn't Marianne, then whom was his dad referring to?

The suspect could be anyone.

The bad feeling in his gut said time was running out.

FIFTEEN

A ringing phone made Bristol jump. She glanced around, and it took her a minute to realize she'd fallen asleep on Chandler's mom's couch. The sun shone through the patio window, telling her more time had passed than she realized.

"This is Chandler." His face grew serious. "On our way." He grabbed his keys and headed for the back door. "Let's go."

"Wait." Bristol tossed the fleece blanket aside and jumped to her feet, clearing the sleep away from her eyes. "Where are we going?"

"That was Josie Hunt."

She shook her head, trying to wake herself. Chandler moved fast, and she had to hurry to catch him. After they climbed into his truck along with Tucker, he pulled out of his mom's drive.

Anticipation built as she could see everything in Chandler's demeanor change. He was in mission mode. She was almost afraid to ask. "What did Josie say?"

He drew a deep breath before he looked at her. "I don't want you to get your hopes up."

"What is it?" Her heart picked up the pace despite his warning.

"She may've found Spencer."

Her breath bottled up in her chest, and her stomach fluttered. "Did she see him? Is he okay? Is he with her?"

Chandler held up his hand. "Slow down. I don't know the details. Our team always calls for backup in these situations, and that's what Josie is doing. All she said was she'd located the white BMW at an abandoned house, and she needed backup."

"But did she see Spencer? You said she may have found him."

"I don't know what we'll find." Softness crossed his features. "Josie said she thought she heard a child. But we don't know if that was Spencer or a neighbor's child or what."

Her hands fisted with anxiety. She lifted her head upward and closed her eyes. "Please, please, God, let us find Spencer, and let him be okay."

As soon as the words were uttered, blood continued to thump in her ears. She glanced at the speedometer. He was going sixty down the paved road, but it seemed like they were crawling. "Can you go faster?"

"I'm hurrying." His hand reached out and grabbed hers. "I'm here for you."

Warmth engulfed her, but nervousness still made her arms shake. He increased the speed a little, but never had a ten-minute drive taken so long. He slowed, passed an old house and then eased down the road before turning around.

"What's wrong?"

"I'm not certain." He pulled into the grassy drive and immediately hit his brakes.

Trees surrounded the abandoned house—what was left of it. A wheat field stood behind the home. The car that had helped run them off the road and onto the train sat to the side underneath the trees and appeared empty. "Where is she?"

"I don't know." He continued to survey the area. "We didn't pass her vehicle on the road."

Concern crinkled around his eyes.

"What is it?"

"Normally, if one of our team members arrives at an unsecure location, we wait for backup. Not wanting to lose the suspects, we'd stay at a safe distance and watch to make certain they didn't leave."

Bristol looked again at their location. The newly planted wheat looked like luscious grass as it blew in the wind behind the old shack. "Do you think she's in the field?"

"I wouldn't think so." He shook his head. "I'm going to check it out."

"Are you taking Tucker with you?"

"Yeah. Come on, boy." He let him out of the truck.

"I'm going, too." She got out and moved beside Chandler.

He whispered, "Remain quiet."

She considered calling Spencer's name, but then she thought better of it.

Her son was close. She could feel it.

Chandler kept hold of Tucker's leash, and the bloodhound put his nose to the ground like he was on the scent of something.

Did he smell Spencer? Did search-and-rescue dogs remember scents?

She picked up the pace, but Chandler's hand shot out. "Wait."

Frustration tugged at her. Patience had all but evaporated, but she did as he asked.

They moved to the white car, several sets of tire

tracks marking the way. Chandler glanced inside and riffled through the console and glove box while she continued to study the house. The frame home's windows were missing, and the roof had caved in. Was her son inside?

"Nothing to indicate who the car belongs to." Chandler drew his gun with one hand while the other retained the leash.

"I wonder if Josie is in the house."

"Could be." His eyebrows drew in as they made their way around the side of the leaning building.

Her shoes stepped on broken boards in the tall grass. Normally she'd watch for snakes, but she was too busy looking for Spencer to pay attention.

At the back corner of the house, the deputy stopped, and his shoulders dropped.

Bristol was quick to move around him so she could see.

The Ford Bronco sat in the back, and someone was inside.

"Josie," Chandler mumbled and hurried toward her. "Who did this to you?"

Was Spencer with her? Hope surfaced, and Bristol ran toward the vehicle.

"Back." The word came out muffled.

What? The words barely registered until she noticed the investigator shaking her head vigorously. But Bristol had already made it to her. "Where's Spencer? Is he here?"

Josie again shook her head, her eyes large. A rag was stuffed in her mouth. This time the muffled words were yelled. "…back!"

Bristol's gaze fell on her hands. They were tied to the steering wheel. She knew in that moment she had rushed into a trap. Too late.

* * *

Chandler yelled, "Get down. Get down!"

He dropped to his haunches. Bristol crawled to the side of the car.

His gaze shot to the grove of trees, but he didn't see movement. He proceeded to his driver's side. His partner's hands were tied to the steering wheel, a grimy rag stuffed in her mouth, and her cheek was smeared with dirt and sported a large bump like someone had hit her.

He hurried to remove the rag and dropped it on the ground while staying low. "Is the suspect still here?"

Josie nodded, her eyes dull, probably from pain. She coughed and gagged. "It was a setup."

Bristol appeared at his side. "Where's my baby?"

Chandler removed a knife from his pocket and quickly cut through the ties that bound his colleague's hands to the steering wheel.

"He…he was here." Josie's dark eyes danced with emotion, and she stammered to get the words out. "I had him in my arms."

"Where is he?" The words flew from Bristol.

Chandler returned the knife to his pocket and didn't give Josie time to answer. "Did you recognize the suspect?"

His partner's eyes grew. "Yeah. He's the—"
Boom!
A single gunshot blasted.

"Get back down." Chandler motioned. Three more shots had Bristol taking cover. Then a blur of a person wearing black raced through the trees. Chandler fired several quick shots. A grunt was his reward, but the man fired again—his aim far to the right—before continuing to run.

"No!" Bristol sprinted toward the truck in his line of fire.

"Get down." Chandler moved away from Josie's Bronco so he wouldn't hit Bristol and got off several more shots.

An engine roared. The maroon truck sped across the field in the opposite direction.

Bristol continued to run after the truck until it disappeared over the hill.

He dropped his gun to his side as she walked back toward him. "What were you thinking? You can't run into the line of fire like that. You're going to get yourself killed."

She threw her hands into the air and yelled, "What difference does it make if I don't get my son back? I was this close." She held her fingers an inch or so apart. Her gaze went to the SUV, and then she swung the driver's door wide. "Josie's been hit."

Chandler's heart stuttered. This couldn't be happening. He quickly called 9-1-1 and relayed the information.

"I found a heartbeat," Bristol said, her face turning pale. "Oh, no. She's bleeding out."

Glancing around to make certain no other gunmen were still there, he hurried to the other side of Josie's vehicle. Blood squirted from just below her rib cage. He put his hand over it and glanced around for the cloth that had been used to gag her. It wasn't in sight. "Is there a rag or towel? Something to stop the bleeding."

"Let me check."

He could hear Bristol digging through the back seat.

"Nothing here." She leaned over the bench seat to the cargo area.

The bleeding was fierce. "Come on, partner. Stay with me."

Josie's eyes fluttered, but he didn't know if she was

aware or not. The color drained from her face, and expressionless eyes stared at him.

"I found this." Bristol shoved what looked to be a beach towel at him.

He folded it and then placed it over the wound. "Stay with me, Josie. Help is on the way."

She blinked, and Bristol returned to the driver's side to be beside her. His partner turned her head. Her lips moved, but the words came out in a mumbled mess.

Chandler's heart constricted. They should've had more backup. He didn't know much about Josie's personal life, but he'd witnessed what she'd done for families of missing children. "Conserve your energy."

Bristol's lip trembled. "What is she trying to tell us?"

Josie tried to speak again.

Bristol glanced up at him. "I can't understand her. Her voice is too weak."

The woman closed her eyes. "Sheriff…"

He and Bristol exchanged looks before Chandler asked, "Did Sheriff Carroll have something to do with the attack?"

Josie's eyes fluttered again, and her right hand clawed at Chandler's arm that held the towel. She tried to answer, but then she went still.

Sirens sounded in the distance. He said, "Go wave them down."

Bristol ran to the country road, and his attention returned to the woman. *Please, God, save her. Don't let her die like my dad. Please.* "Josie, help is here. Stay strong. We need you on this team."

He continued spouting words, uncertain if she could hear him. Anything to give her encouragement, for you never knew if a person was conscious or not. Seconds later, an ambulance and a deputy's car pulled through the drive. Chandler stayed with her, continuing to keep pressure on the wound.

"I've got it. Move away." A young female paramedic tugged on the back of Chandler's shirt.

When he released the pressure, he noted blood saturated the towel, making his stomach swirl. "Hurry."

Deputy Perkins walked up, worry etched across her face. Thankfully, she didn't say anything, for Chandler didn't trust his voice wouldn't give way to the emotion.

The deputy was in deep conversation with Bristol when another car pulled into the drive. Chandler recognized Archie, one of paramedics from the daycare van crash site. The brawny man hurried over to the other worker. "How can I help?"

The emergency responder glanced at Archie and then started giving instructions.

Sheriff Carroll's car pulled into the drive. Distrust twisted Chandler's gut. What had his partner been trying to say? Had the sheriff been here? Was that how he'd gotten here so fast? As the man climbed out of his vehicle, Chandler schooled his features, trying to hide the suspicion he now held.

"What's going on, Murphy?"

Chandler drew a deep breath. *Don't let the sheriff know you suspect him.* "Josie Hunt's been shot. She'd called us for backup, and when we got here, she was strapped into her car, her hands tied to the steering wheel. When Bristol and I moved in to help her, someone fired a shot, hitting her. It was the same suspect that abducted the daycare children. I fired several rounds but don't know if any hit the mark."

The sheriff's eyebrows drew in. "Did Hunt say who did this to her?"

Did she name you as the suspect? A couple of seconds passed while Chandler tamped down the accusations running through his mind. He had to play this right. Needed a solid case before he voiced his thoughts. If the sheriff was behind the attack, why? What did he have to do with Bristol's son? "She mentioned Spencer was still alive."

The sheriff's jaw twitched. "That's good news."

"Sir, I'd like to pursue the suspect," Chandler said.

The sheriff rubbed the back of his neck. "I think it's time we bring in a couple more deputies to help you."

Did the sheriff just want to keep tabs on him?

Bristol moved beside him.

The sheriff continued, "I'm going to put Deputy Sample and Deputy Reynolds on the case, too."

Chandler suddenly didn't want any deputy on the case for fear he or she would keep the sheriff in the loop. Sample and Reynolds were fine, but more inexperienced. He couldn't think of a way to phrase it where he wouldn't appear suspicious.

Archie came over. "Just wanted to let you know, care flight should be here shortly. This one's going to need more trauma expertise than what Liberty Memorial can offer."

"Thanks, Archie. You've been a big help." Chandler moved to the group of deputies and gave them a brief update. The other two were already familiar with the case, but it didn't hurt to go over everything again. He answered a couple of questions, and when he glanced at Bristol, she was staring off into the distance, swinging her arms back and forth. He got it. He felt the same anxiety.

This guy needed to be caught. Today.

Sheriff Carroll had been standing off to the side, seemingly in deep thought. Now he joined them. "Hawkins, I want you to head north, checking houses and talking to the people. Deputy Green, I want you to head south and do the same. Murphy, I need you to stay here and answer questions and make certain we didn't miss any evidence."

The sheriff's word hit Chandler like a sucker punch to the gut. He couldn't do this. After the others dispersed, he approached the man. "Sheriff, I'd like to track the suspect. He took Bristol's son, and now he shot Josie Hunt. I can't stand back and let the others do the work."

The sheriff put his hand on Chandler's shoulder. "I figured you'd feel that way, son. But I believe you're more important here. The chance of finding the suspect by driving around is low right now. What I need is someone who's familiar with the case to be leading it. Guiding the others. You know who to talk to. What to look for. You're more valuable here. Help search for more evidence that will tell us who the suspect is. Then you can follow up the leads."

Chandler stared at the man for several silent seconds. Did the sheriff really believe that was the best course, or was he trying to keep Chandler off the trail for fear it'd lead back to Carroll? Chandler had told no one Josie's last words. "Yes, sir."

Anger boiled through him, making the pent-up energy nearly explode. He watched as the sheriff stared after Archie, the paramedic, and then glanced around the property before getting into his vehicle and driving away.

Bristol approached him. "Are you ready to go?"

He hated to tell her what he'd been instructed to do. "I'm being ordered to stay here to look for evidence and help the others. The sheriff wants to find out who's behind these attacks."

Her eyes squinted, and he expected her to argue or blow up, but Bristol just nodded. "Okay."

When she turned to walk away, his hand shot out and touched her shoulder. "This is not what I wanted."

"I didn't figure it was. I heard Josie's words."

He blinked. "Bristol, we don't know that the sheriff's behind this. Don't jump to conclusions."

"As if you're not?" Her eyebrows shot up. "I'm going to find my son. I can't stand around."

"I'm doing the best I can." He hated the frustration in his own voice, but she needed to hear it.

She glanced back. "I'm not blaming you. My son's life is on the line."

Like a concrete block tied around his foot in a swift-running river, no matter how hard he concentrated, how hard he tried, he continued to sink deeper. Bristol needed him, and he intended to do everything in his power to protect her while finding her son. "Bristol, wait up. You can ride with me. I'll take you where you need to go."

SIXTEEN

Bristol wasn't certain she wanted to ride with Chandler. He had a boss to listen to and rules to go by. This she understood, but she couldn't take the chance he'd be removed from the case. Maybe she should've hitched a ride with Deputy Perkins.

Chandler turned up the radio. Voices of the other deputies came across the air, but from what they said, no one had spotted the pickup yet.

"Do you think the sheriff is behind the attacks?"

He stared straight ahead. "I don't know. I've been thinking about that. Why would he?"

"I don't know. Why does anyone hurt others? Greed, or they have something to hide."

He turned the radio lower and looked at her. "What would the sheriff have to gain by taking a three-year-old boy?"

"Same as anyone else. Leverage?"

"But Rex is Spencer's dad. Seems to me the leverage would only be against his mom or dad. Do you have anything the sheriff would want?"

"No. I feel like I've answered this question multiple times. Besides turning evidence against Rex and a couple of his friends to the sheriff, I don't even know the lawman. He was cordial when I came in and then I left town. That's all I know."

Chandler drove toward the main highway but kept his speed down. "You mentioned friends. Did they go to prison like Rex?"

She stared at him. "Wait—didn't we already discuss this?" She noted how his expression fell. "You know. Are you testing me? Trying to catch me in a lie or something?"

"Of course not. I want you to tell me in your own words."

"No, Deputy Murphy. That's not it. I can't trust you. Sorry. I thought I could."

"Look, it's not that." He turned onto the main highway headed toward Liberty and eased into traffic. "Josie mentioned the sheriff but didn't get to complete her sentence. I'm trying to make sense of it. I'm missing something. But what? I'll be honest with you if you're honest with me."

She frowned and crossed her arms. "I'm not hiding anything."

"I already knew you turned evidence against your husband," he said matter-of-factly.

"Ex-husband."

"Ex-husband. Even though you were supposed to be anonymous, I still learned you turned Rex and a couple of friends in."

"So…if you knew, so did others. Whoever has Spencer could be connected to Victor or Barry Blackburn. But I already guessed that. Barry only served a year in prison, and Victor is still inside. But why am I telling you? You were there."

He nodded. "I was."

Realization hit her, and her stomach tightened. "I

suppose you also know about me transporting the drugs across the border?"

"That, too." He reached across the console, but she jerked her hand away before he could touch her.

"Don't." Irritation bit at her. "It's not like I did it on purpose or that I kept it from authorities."

"Bristol, I realize that. I was just wondering if anyone else should be on that list. Someone that you haven't thought of."

"Yes, of course. Someone whose first name starts with an *M*. I've been racking my brain trying to figure out who took my soon and tried to kill me. Us."

"Did you know my father?"

She glanced up at him, the question surprising her. "No. Only that he had been investigating Rex."

"Your ex never mentioned him?"

She shook her head. "My husband didn't confide in me. Ever. When we were dating and first married, I accepted everything he said at face value. It wasn't until he got violent and let his ugly side show that I realized he wasn't everything he seemed to be."

Dark eyes watched her, seemingly taking in her very being. "That's a shame. I'm sorry, Bristol. You deserved better."

Emotion clogged her throat. She waited a moment for the feeling to go away. "If I knew anything that would help you solve your dad's disappearance, I would tell you."

"It's been bothering me ever since Anthony mentioned Sheriff Carroll asking about my dad's body—as if he knows he's dead."

Bristol caught his meaning. "Not like he assumes it, but knows…"

"Right." Chandler's phone dinged. He glanced down at the text and then held it out for Bristol to read. "I knew it."

Photo's a fake. Image of Dad is from an award ceremony taken nine months before he disappeared.

"That's good news."

"Yeah. I knew it must be, but for a moment…"

"You hoped he was still alive?"

"Exactly." He turned to her. "Want to see what the sheriff is doing?"

"What?" She sat straight in her seat.

"I don't know where else to look. *MC* was in my dad's notes. I don't know what the *M* stands for, but the *C* could stand for *Carroll*. Someone had photos of my dad from the department. Anthony mentioned the sheriff. Josie Hunt said his name. And he didn't want me going to look for the suspect."

Anticipation flowed through Bristol, giving her chills. "Let's go see what your boss is doing." For the first time since this nightmare began, she believed they were about to learn something big.

Chandler parked his truck down from the sheriff's mom's house. It had been easy to learn the man's whereabouts. One call to the station to ask to speak to the sheriff, and Joyner, the deputy pulling desk duty, told him their boss wasn't in but had gone to his mom's.

He and Bristol had been sitting there for just under an hour at the end of the street, watching. The sheriff had arrived about forty-five minutes ago. Several times someone had passed by a window, but Chandler couldn't make out their identity. Once, an older lady let a dog out the door for a few minutes and then let him back in.

Finally, the sheriff reappeared at the door. He yelled back inside, his words unintelligible, and then strode to his truck. If he noticed Chandler's truck parked down the street, he didn't show any reaction. They waited while he fiddled with something in his truck—probably his cell phone—and then he pulled away from the curb and drove up the street.

Chandler needed to be careful not to give away his position, so he waited until the sheriff was a block up the road before putting his truck into gear.

Suddenly, the door to the house opened, and Archie, the paramedic and the sheriff's brother, jogged around to the back of the house, and two seconds later, his sports car pulled down the drive.

"That's the car!" Bristol pointed.

"The one you saw at Tito's place?"

"Yeah."

The red Dodge Charger pulled onto the road and sped off.

"Wonder what his hurry is," Chandler mumbled. Torn, he took off in the same direction as both vehicles. "Which one do you think I should follow?"

"The paramedic has been nothing but helpful, but something makes me think he's the one to watch."

"I agree." With no time to consider his actions, he followed Archie's sports car instead of the sheriff's SUV. He tailed him to the edge of town and onto the main highway, headed away from Liberty. The paramedic's taillights grew smaller, and Chandler was forced to pick up speed for fear of losing him. Maybe Archie realized the sheriff was deep in this case and wanted to intervene.

"He was at the scene where the daycare van crashed.

He gave Mr. Hewitt CPR. He's the sheriff's brother, right?"

Chandler's mind cleared with the possibilities. "Yeah. And he was off duty when Josie Hunt was shot but got there within minutes."

Bristol's eyes grew wide. "You're right. How did he get there so fast? Why was he with the sheriff? You think they're in cahoots?"

"Good question."

As he hurried to stay up with the car, he racked his brain. "If Archie is involved, the initials still don't match my dad's notes."

"True." She gripped her door and leaned forward.

The farther he followed Archie out of town, the more Chandler was certain even if Archie wasn't the man behind the kidnapping, he at least participated. Their speeds built, in excess of ninety miles per hour. Had they been spotted?

Not knowing if the sheriff could be trusted, he called Bliss, the founder of Bring the Children Home Project, and explained the situation. Then he called Deputy Perkins, whom he knew he could trust.

Chandler explained that he was following Archie and needed backup from her and Deputy Green. "Do you know anything about Archie?"

"Not really. Just that he's the sheriff's brother and that they had a falling-out years ago."

He blew out a breath. "I never knew that."

"I'm not surprised. Unless they're working the same scene, they don't have much to do with one another, and the sheriff doesn't mention him much."

"Thanks." He hung up and looked at Bristol, but she was leaning forward and staring out the window. The road snaked through the trees, and long shadows covered the road.

"You think the sheriff is covering for his brother?"

He frowned. "Could be."

Her face lit up. "I recognize where we are."

"Where?"

"There's a cabin out here that Rex used to stay at when he claimed to go fishing or hunting."

"Claimed to go?"

"Yeah. I was so naive. I even encouraged him to relax and take a break from work. I came here once to surprise him, but instead of fishing, I found him with another woman. It wasn't until later that I learned of more affairs. There was no telling how many other meeting places he had."

His fists tightened at what Rex had done to Bristol. "Not all men are like that."

"I realize that." She stared straight ahead. "Spencer is at that cabin."

Chandler looked at her.

She turned to him. "I can feel it. I'm praying I can bring him home tonight."

Chandler absorbed her statement. This was the second time she'd mentioned prayer. As a child, he'd always been taken to worship services. It pleased him she, too, followed God. *Please, Lord, let her be right. Help us find her son today. And if it be Your will, let us learn what happened to my dad.*

He hadn't gone to worship services since his dad disappeared. Although not as often, he still prayed. Seeing Sydney getting her life straight and the example of Bristol's faith encouraged him. He realized he'd done himself no favors by not leaning on God more.

The red convertible was no longer in sight, but there

wasn't much down this road. Tree limbs hung low, almost covering the entrance, but he saw it at the last minute.

"This is it." Bristol leaned forward and pointed. "Turn here."

He hit his brakes. Tall grass and weeds lined the entrance, and the grass was beaten down, indicating someone had recently passed this way. His truck dipped and bounced with every bump on the trail. A shallow wash crossed the path in front of them, and he gassed it. His truck slid sideways, and mud flung from the spinning tires.

He tried to keep his speed down so as to not draw attention, and the mud didn't make it easy, but fresh tracks let him know he'd gone the right way.

After a moment of fearing his truck would get stuck, he gained traction and made it to the other side. It didn't look like the place had run cattle or been tilled in many years. Green grass shoved its way through the brush from the previous year. A thick line of trees formed on the right, and another small wash appeared in front of him. As he came out on the other side, an enclosed clearing appeared in front of him. Through the trees, he spotted a cabin.

"This is it. I'm ready to get my son."

He grabbed her hand. "I don't know what we'll find here, but if Archie is behind the kidnapping, he'll be ready, and we have no backup yet. Do you understand?"

"We're taking a chance?" Her blue eyes bored into his. "I'll be careful. But I'll also do everything in my power to rescue him. No matter the cost."

Chandler was glad to hear her say that. He'd just been thinking the same thing. About her.

SEVENTEEN

Several minutes passed while Bristol sat in Chandler's borrowed truck, waiting for him to gather his gun and ammunition. Her heart drummed in her chest, and she drew a deep breath, preparing herself for what was to come.

"I think I have everything." He eyed her. "Do you have your gun?"

"Ready." The .45 rested in her ankle holster. Not knowing if she'd see Spencer first or have to defend herself, she thought it best to keep it close.

"Deputies Perkins, Joyner and Green are on their way."

"Are you sure we have to wait?" Patience was not her strong point, and believing her son was close could make the calmest mother crack. "We're both armed."

He took her hand again. "I want this to go smoothly. No mistakes. No chances taken. If Spencer is in the cabin, he'll be safer the more law enforcement is here."

Crash!

The noise came from the woods, and they both looked at one another.

"What was that?" Her eyebrows arched.

"Let me check it out." He attached Tucker's leash to the harness. "Come on, boy."

Tucker leaped out of the truck, and Chandler came around to her side. She rolled down the window.

"I want you to stay here. If anything goes wrong, take my truck and head to the cutoff five miles back and wait for the deputies." He leaned in and gave her a kiss on the cheek before turning around and disappearing into the brush with the dog.

"Be careful." She mumbled the words. Her cheek still tingled as she rolled up the window. She scooted over the console to the driver's seat in case she needed to leave in a hurry. A minute passed, and there was no sign of Chandler or anyone else. The wind blowing through the trees was the only sound.

That was a good sign, right? It must've been a limb or something falling in the trees.

She couldn't believe he'd kissed her. Not that she didn't find him attractive, because she did, but she didn't want a relationship. When all this was over and Spencer was safe in her home, she would think about her future. Rex was dead, and she was almost through with her teaching degree. Was there more?

Could she trust herself not to make the same poor decisions she had made with Rex?

Movement outside by the large oak grabbed her attention. Chandler let his gun drop to his side as he headed back to the truck. Relief flooded her. False alarm.

He shrugged like he didn't know what the sound was from.

Boom!

Chandler dropped to the ground, and a dog yelped.

A black Chevy pickup flew up the trail and skidded to a stop beside her door.

Disbelief slammed into her as she stared into her ex-husband's smiling face. *Rex!*

He carried Spencer in his arms. Her son was kicking and crying.

She withdrew her gun from the holster, but Rex ripped open the door, holding their son in front of him.

"Miss me, darling? You better give me that gun." He held out his hand.

"Mama!"

Her heart stopped for a split second, trying to make sense of it. But she couldn't give up. Not this time.

Spencer's cry forced her into action. Instead of giving her ex what he asked for, she aimed the gun at Rex's head. "No! Put Spencer down, or I'll shoot."

Rex gave her an incredulous stare, momentarily caught off guard. "You've gotten too big for your britches…"

When he moved for her, she shot above his head to make certain she didn't hit Spencer.

Please don't make me shoot you in front of our son.

But her ex still flinched. He moved toward her while Spencer screamed. Another shot blew out the windshield, and the bullet whizzed past her head. As she looked up to see where the shot came from, Rex grabbed her by the bicep and yanked her out of the truck, causing her to stumble.

A powerful kick to her hand sent pain throughout her being, but she clung to the gun like her life depended on it. The throbbing made it difficult to grip the butt of the gun.

Rex bared his teeth and his nostrils flared as he reared back and came down with a pistol on top of her hand.

This time her gun skittered to the ground. He held his own pistol and shoved it into her belly. "I won't even hesitate to pull the trigger. If you want to live another second, get into my truck."

He shoved her in the back.

She had no choice but to do his bidding. Spencer lunged at her as they hurried toward his vehicle. A glimpse in the direction Chandler had gone down, and she barely had time to see his body before Rex shoved her again. "Move!"

He held the driver's door open. "Get in."

He was letting her drive? She climbed in, and he ran around to the passenger side with the gun pointed at her. He got in, holding Spencer.

"No!" Spencer clawed at Rex, trying to get out of his grasp.

"Go."

She hit the gas and took off, afraid he'd hurt Spencer if she didn't.

"Let me go." Spencer shoved against Rex's chest.

"Settle down." Rex gave him a shake and then turned to her, anger flashing in his eyes. "Tell him to shut up."

"Don't hurt him," she warned her ex. "Spencer, honey, relax. Be quiet for Mommy."

As she drove through the trees, another gunshot went off. She looked in her rearview mirror but couldn't see Chandler.

Please, Lord, let him be okay.

Her son's lips puckered as he fought Rex's grasp. Fear and hurt shone in his eyes, and her heart broke. But she had to control the situation as much as she could and not let fear reign. She'd changed since she'd sneaked away in the middle of the night years ago. She was no coward or a victim. If there was any way possible, she intended to walk away from this madman with their son.

She drew a few deep breaths to calm her nerves.

"Turn left." Rex spit the command with excited eagerness.

Although she didn't glance his way, she could see the smirk on his lips in her peripheral vision. The question if people were evil used to cross her mind. Maybe some people couldn't help themselves. But seeing Rex again confirmed her belief that he enjoyed being mean. He didn't fight it, to her knowledge, but reveled in hurting others. After all, until he had hidden the drugs in her coat and she turned him in, she'd done nothing to deserve his anger.

And poor Spencer surely had done nothing to deserve this treatment. Did the man not have a heart?

"Turn right at the next road."

They passed a dilapidated sign, but the letters were so worn it couldn't be read. There was no need to. She remembered where they were. This was close to one of the concrete plants Rex had spent time at. Once her husband had forgotten his lunch, and she decided to take him a box of fish and fries—one of his favorites—since it was his birthday. Instead of being grateful, he'd accused her of checking up on him.

Overgrown ditches lined both sides of the road, and an old cement mixer drum sat in the weeds, announcing the place hadn't been used in years. A cinder-block building with part of the roof caved in stood in the middle, and like everything else, weeds and tree saplings surrounded the place. A group of three tall silos towered off to the side, and a few pieces of rusted equipment lay scattered in the back.

A pit developed in her stomach. No one would ever find her out here if she disappeared.

"Stop." Rex got out, ran around the truck and punched

a keypad. The rusty metal gate opened. He hurried back into the cab. "Go."

She did as he asked and pulled up to the building.

Please, God, be with me. Help me make smart decisions. And please be with Chandler. I don't know what happened to him.

"Get out."

Rex's harsh command had her heart pounding, but she continued to pray as she stepped out.

What was his plan?

"Follow me. And know if you try anything, I won't hesitate to hurt the boy. You wouldn't like that, would you?"

Bile came into her throat, and she swallowed it before she got sick. No doubt he'd hurt their son to get even with her, and she didn't dare take the chance.

The old building stood in front of them, and he took long strides toward it—a man excited about his mission. Shadows swallowed the area and she waited for her eyes to adjust before the room came into view. A large metal desk was crammed against the far wall with an outdated-looking computer system on it. Grimy shelves held a couple of notebooks, and a metal chair leaned to one side.

Rex put Spencer in the chair and bent down. "Don't move, little Rex. Daddy will be right back."

Nausea burned in her stomach. *Little Rex?* He wanted Spencer to be just like him. Like father, like son. Spencer was still young enough that if something happened to her and Rex got away with him, her son would never remember her. He wouldn't be taught right from wrong.

She couldn't let that happen.

Rex's brown, sinister eyes turned on her. "Outside... unless you want the boy to watch."

A lump formed in her throat that she couldn't swallow.

"No. No. No." Spencer ran toward her, but Rex caught him by the back of his shirt and spun him around.

"Oh, no, you don't. Here, eat this." He tossed a stick of gum at him and then turned to her. "You thought you were pretty clever, turning me in and then running. I told you, baby, don't ever cross me. But you didn't listen. Now you must pay the price."

Her instinct told her to run, but one glance into her son's fearful eyes and she knew she couldn't leave him there with his criminal father. A bulge in the side of his waistband showed his gun was still on him, but he wielded a large knife in his hand. A gun would be too fast. He intended to savor every second of killing her. "Out the door, sweetheart."

Time had run out. She did as he asked, and as she descended the steps outside the building, her gaze continued to look for something to use as a weapon. A metal bar, a stick, a rock—anything. But there was nothing close by except for leaves and a few twigs littering the ground. Rex continued prodding her to the side of the building.

A dozer-like machine stood on the crumbling pavement—one with a bucket on the front for moving materials. Her eyes lit on a freshly dug hole about two feet deep and eight feet long.

A grave. *My grave.*

Tingling surfaced as a scream bubbled in the back of her throat. This couldn't be happening. No matter what she'd done to free herself from this man, her demise stood in front of her, mocking her. She'd lost everything.

The blade poked into her back. "Get in."

"No." She jerked in his grasp even as the blade nicked her between the shoulder blades. Even though she'd watched countless self-defense videos, she'd never gotten to practice on anyone, and all advice vanished from her mind. All she could think was that she must get away at all costs.

She jerked and kicked, not caring if the knife cut her. Her arm slipped in Rex's grasp. As he tried to regain control by squeezing her wrist, she drove her head into his chest, causing him to lose his balance.

His curses filled the air as they tumbled to the crumbling concrete slab, tangled in each other's grasp. She continued in a frenzy of kicks and punches. *Fight, Bristol!* Over and over she repeated the words in her mind.

Fury lit on his face, his brown eyes flashing a hate she'd never witnessed. With pure determination, she jabbed her finger into his eye as hard as she could. He growled in pain, and she scrambled to her feet.

She took off in an all-out run across the uneven ground. Heavy footsteps and breathing sounded behind her, egging her on. A narrow ditch appeared in front of her. As she went to leap it, he tackled her from behind, knocking her to the ground, hard.

This time, the end of the barrel of his gun slammed into the side of her neck.

"Please, please, try that again. My patience is gone. Do exactly as I say. Your boy is watching every move."

She glanced over her shoulder. Spencer stood on the platform, his eyes wide with fear. Defeat collapsed in on her, determination slipping away. She tried to find the stubbornness that had driven her over the past four years, but what cost was she willing to pay?

Her voice came out shaky. "Okay. I'll do as you say. Don't hurt me in front of my son."

Chandler writhed in pain. The bullet had hit him in the thigh and went straight through. Although it didn't lodge, blood flowed down his leg and soaked his pants. But he had to move. He'd recognized Rex Edwards as the first shooter.

The second shooter had been Archie, but Chandler had taken him out of action as he moved through the trees to see if Chandler was still alive. A quick check on the paramedic showed he was breathing but in serious condition.

Resolve forced Chandler into action. Rex was going down.

Chandler stripped off his polo shirt, leaving him in a black tee. He folded the polo lengthwise before wrapping it around his thigh. Tucker whimpered and sniffed his leg. "I'm okay, Tuck." He nuzzled the dog's back with his arm so he could stretch the shirt. It still wouldn't tie around his leg. He clenched it tightly in place and hobbled back to the cabin with Tucker at his side. He quickly grabbed a sheet from the bed and ripped it in half. After securing the cloth around the wound, he hurried to his vehicle and allowed his dog to jump in first.

He first dialed 9-1-1 for Archie Carroll. Then he put a call in to Joyner as he tore out the drive. "Have you learned anything new?"

"Yes. I heard from the investigators. McGinnis, the inmate that was supposed to be released from Huntsville the week before Rex, has not be seen from his family. Investigators are looking into the possibility of him being the one who was cremated. That means Rex may be alive."

"He is." He gave Joyner an abbreviated version of the situation. Joyner already knew the cabin's location, so Chandler didn't repeat it. "Did you find any locations of Warner Concrete plants around here?"

"I already told you, the closest plant is over forty miles away."

"Look again. We've already checked those out."

"Wait. What is this?"

"What?"

"There's a plant off Sutton Drive. Uh, hold on." He heard the clicking of the keyboard. "Looks to be about six miles from you." He rattled off the address.

"I know where that's at. What deputies are on the way?"

"I sent them all. Including Sheriff Carroll." He paused, and when Chandler didn't respond, he said, "Murphy, be careful."

Chandler clicked off and turned left on the country road. He prayed that was where Rex had taken Bristol and that Chandler wouldn't be too late.

He shoved the agony to the back of his mind as he sped down the rock road, dust kicking high into the air. His gun was ready. Tucker looked out the window and then turned to him and whimpered. The dog must've sensed, driving this speed, that something was going on. He turned down one road and then another.

Where was she?

He continued at a ridiculously fast speed, keeping a lookout for other vehicles, but saw no one.

Finally, he came to a metal-pipe gate that crossed a wide entrance. This was it. As he pulled in, his gaze landed on the abandoned building of the concrete plant—

and Spencer standing on the tall concrete platform. A front-end loader bounced across the pavement with its bucket raised.

Rex sat behind the controls.

Where was Bristol? He had to find her, but she was nowhere in sight.

Chandler backed up to get a running start and slammed on the gas. Rocks spewed from his tires as he shot across the culvert and crashed into the gate. The barrier bent and swung open as the lock gave way. He flew across the yard.

He slid to a stop near the front-end loader just as a bullet came through his windshield and lodged in the seat beside him. He ducked, grabbed his gun and shoved the door open. Using the door as a shield, he got out and peeked through the window, searching for Bristol.

He sucked in a breath as he saw a hand swing into the air. She was in the hole. Anger rocked him as the bucket full of wet concrete poured out on top of her. *No!*

Firing his gun at Rex, Chandler sprinted across the pavement as fast as his injured leg would allow. The thug returned fire, bullets whizzing all around Chandler as he made it to the stairs. It wasn't much protection, but was better than nothing.

Chandler glanced up at Spencer. "Go back inside. I'll help your mom."

The boy's lips puckered, but he did as he was told.

Chandler fired two more shots, one hitting Rex in the shoulder as Chandler ran for the hole. The bulky piece of equipment stood between him and Bristol, so he had to skirt wide. Rex turned in the seat and fired again, but his aim was off.

Several sheriff's deputies pulled into the yard.

As Chandler drew closer, he could barely see Bristol, her body submerged in the concrete. The hole must've been deep. No doubt the rocks and sand made the liquid heavy and difficult to escape. Not only was the chance of drowning a threat, but the concrete would cause burns if she didn't get out soon. There was no time to hesitate.

Chandler moved closer, but gunshots made him take cover behind a tree. As bullets sprayed, wood splintered into the air. He caught Deputy Perkins's attention and pointed to the office.

Perkins ran upstairs to where Spencer was hiding, and the other deputies crouched behind their vehicles.

Chandler glanced back at the hole. Bristol was barely above the surface. He couldn't wait another second. *Please, God, protect me.* He sprinted for the hole and lay on the ground, his hand searching for Bristol. After one swipe and touching nothing, he leaned farther into the hole, his chest dipping into the concrete, and his hand touched something—her arm.

A massive shadow passed over him, and the ground shook. He looked up. The bucket of the loader hovered above. He dodged just as the massive yellow machine crashed down.

Several rounds of gunfire went off.

The bucket hit the ground, barely missing him but causing him to lose his grip on Bristol. He quickly snatched her arm again and tugged her upward. He scrambled to his feet and continued to pull until she was above the surface. Concrete sludge dripped from her body, and he dragged her away from the edge.

A glance at the loader showed Rex slumped forward over the controls. Deputies rushed their way as Chandler swiped the slurry away from Bristol's face. "Bristol, can you hear me?"

She didn't respond. He dropped to his knees, ready to perform CPR, but she coughed. He paused, and her eyes blinked. She shook her head and swiped at her mouth, gasping for air and trying to clear her throat.

A paramedic appeared at his side. "We've got this. Get back."

Chandler didn't want to release his grip on her hand, but he realized the paramedics knew what to do.

As he stood back and watched, the team of EMTs placed a bottle of something to her lips. Another medic showed up, and the three of them blocked Chandler's view. He prayed earnestly, like he'd never prayed before. *Please save her, Lord.*

For what seemed like an eternity, he watched helplessly as the team worked on her.

Words like *Keep washing* and *Her lungs are clear* floated to him.

"You're gagging me." Bristol's voice came out garbled, but it was her voice.

Those were the most beautiful words Chandler had ever heard.

"I need to look at that." A paramedic pointed at his thigh.

"I'm fine."

The man, who was in his fifties, shook his head. "No, you're not. Come lie down on this stretcher." Chandler did as he was asked, but his concern remained with Bristol.

Sheriff Carroll showed up at his side. "You did good, Murphy. Your father would be proud."

Chandler looked at his boss for a hint of guilt, but sympathy, and something else, showed in his eyes. Guilt?

Those words meant more to him than anyone knew. But right now, he needed Bristol to be okay. She'd become more important to him than he had thought possible.

EIGHTEEN

Bristol looked at the paramedics and glanced around, trying to orient herself. Her clothes were soaked, and she was freezing. "Why am I so wet?"

A lady said, "We washed the cement off you. Keep the blanket on."

She tried to clear the cobwebs from her brain. "Where's Spencer?"

Chandler strode to her. "It's all right. Spencer is safe with Hattie."

"Where's Rex?"

"He's been shot, Bristol."

She blinked. "Is he…dead?"

Chandler touched her hand. "Yeah."

Her chest constricted at the words. "I didn't want him to die, but I didn't want him to hurt us, either."

A comforting smile formed on his lips. "I know what you mean. We're still sorting through the details."

She sat on the stretcher. "I want to see my son."

"He's upstairs." Chandler jerked his head toward the block building. "Can you make it up there?"

"Yes."

The EMT shook her head and exchanged the blanket for a warm one. "Ma'am, we need you to remain where you are."

Hattie came down the stairs and crossed the yard with Spencer on her hip. "That's okay. Stay where you are."

"Mama!" Spencer wiggled his way from Hattie's grasp and ran to Bristol. He wrapped his arms around her neck.

She pulled him close and closed her eyes. "You're all right. Mama's got you."

"We'll need to transport you to the hospital," the paramedic said. She turned to Chandler. "And that goes for you, too, Deputy."

"Yes, ma'am." Chandler nodded.

Hattie said, "I'll take Spencer and meet you at the hospital, if it's all right with you."

"Thank you." Bristol gave her son another hug and held him for just a moment longer. "Go with Hattie. I'll see you in a bit."

"No." His face wrinkled into a frown, and he clung to her. "I go with you."

Chandler turned to the paramedic. "Can the boy ride in the ambulance if Hattie rides along?"

The woman looked at him and smiled. "There should be room."

"Thanks." Chandler knelt beside Bristol. "Are you going to be okay?"

Her heart melted at the sight of Chandler covered in muck and the temporary bandage on his leg. For a moment, emotion clogged her throat. "I have my son back, and Rex can no longer hurt us. I owe it all to you. I couldn't have done this alone. Thank you. I'll never have to look over my shoulder again, no matter where I go."

Chandler's gaze searched hers, and he pulled her

hand into his, warmth enveloping her. "You need to let them take you to the hospital, and then we'll talk."

What was he saying? His soft expression had her wondering if he meant more than catching up on the case.

The paramedic said, "Sir, you need to step back."

Chandler kissed her hand and then mouthed, "We need to talk."

"I'd like that, too." When the paramedics started to move her on the stretcher, she convinced them to let her walk. She had rested enough to feel better and hated being helpless. Clutching the blanket against the chill, she stepped into the ambulance. She rode in the back, and Hattie sat across from her and held Spencer. One of the medics continued to check her vitals and kept her occupied on the transport. Even though Spencer was only a foot away, her hand stayed glued to his leg. She didn't think she could ever let him out of her sight again. Not for a while, anyway.

"You're good for him."

"Who?" She glanced at Hattie. "Spencer?"

The deputy chuckled. "Chandler. I've never seen him this consumed with anyone in the years I've known him."

"I don't know what you're talking about. He's just helping with this case, probably because he believes Rex is responsible for his father's disappearance."

"It's more than that. And if I had to guess, I'd say you feel the same about him."

Bristol thought about what the woman had said. Was it really that obvious?

But Chandler was just helping her. Right? After Rex, she'd decided to never jump into a relationship quickly again. But here she was, allowing Chandler to consume her thoughts. Was it possible her judgment had improved? Or maybe Chandler was for real. That thought scared her. She'd been afraid to indulge in hope for a long time, if ever. Did she dare?

Chandler was antsy to get to the hospital to see Bristol and have his leg tended to, but it was one interruption after another.

"I think we found something," Deputy Joyner hollered.

All the others gathered around, including Chandler. Deputy Green asked, "What is it?"

A piece of rough concrete had chipped off the pad in front of the batch office, and a crack split the slab down the middle. "Looks like another grave, and the loader must've broken it up. I'm not certain, but that looks like a wristwatch."

Chandler held his breath, and his chest tightened. But even as he wondered at the find, he knew what they'd found. His dad's grave. He and Sydney had given their dad the watch several years ago for Father's Day.

A strange feeling enveloped him. This was what he'd wanted, right? To have closure. But with closure, hope disappeared. Was he ready for that? Now his family could complete the grieving process and move on, like his dad would've wanted. After five years of trying to solve the case, it was over. Now maybe he could move on, too.

"The grave's a little big for one person," Deputy Joyner suggested. "Unless the hole was here for something else to do with the plant."

Sheriff Carroll frowned. "Concrete plants normally have a stormwater pit. But that looks like two graves.

We won't know for certain until we get an autopsy, but this concrete is darker, indicating it's older."

The sheriff moved over and rested his hand on Chandler's shoulder. "The department lost a good man with your father. I miss him, son."

Emotion clogged his throat, and Chandler remained quiet, absorbing the sheriff's words. His dad had been a good man. Even though they'd had disagreements typical to families, he loved his dad. Extracting him from the slab would take a while and was something he didn't want to witness. The urge to get to the hospital was still strong. He told the sheriff, and the man agreed he should leave.

Deputy Green walked out of the batch office, the room where the concrete was dispensed into the trucks by computer, and waved at Chandler to come up.

He climbed the steps, his leg getting sorer by the minute. "What is it?"

"Joyner found this in a hole in the wall behind the desk." His gloved hands held out an envelope with several pieces of paper and photos.

Wearing gloves, Chandler glanced through the photos and stopped when he got to a photo of a younger and slimmer Archie Carroll, the sheriff's brother. The image was of the porch on an old house, and Archie was taking a bag from a known drug dealer. On the back was a handwritten date of six years ago. There was also a list of people, several of whom had criminal records, mainly with drugs and one who was doing time for homicide. The implications were obvious, but the evidence would take time to sift through. But it made sense. Rex had to have a contact on the outside to help execute Spencer's kidnapping. If Archie was dealing, it would make the perfect blackmail to get the paramedic to help.

Chandler inhaled a deep breath and walked over to the sheriff.

"I want you to take care of that injury." The sheriff rubbed his bicep, a telltale sign he didn't like what he was about to say. "You need to know I was investigating Archie. I had no idea how deep in trouble he'd gotten himself, or that he helped with the kidnapping. If I'd known—"

"Archie is responsible for his own actions."

Carroll frowned. "I wish I could've done more."

"I understand." Chandler had no more power over Sydney than the sheriff did over his brother, but he intended to do everything he could to repair his relationship with his sister. She had come a long way, and he planned to be a better brother. "I'm going to the hospital now."

"Take care of that injury, and we'll talk later."

He nodded and then hurried to his truck. He couldn't get to the hospital fast enough.

When he arrived, the nurse informed him Bristol was being observed but should be released soon. He knocked before entering her room. Bristol's hair hung down, wet, like she'd just showered. Her gaze went to him. Spencer lay in the bed beside her, sound asleep.

"Hey, good-looking."

She laughed, almost a snort. "Oh, please."

Seeing her smile lit up his world. He leaned over the bed and kissed her on the lips. "I'm so relieved you're going to be okay."

Her eyes glistened. "Me, too. I'm ready to get out of this place and spend time with him." She gave a whimsical smile at her sleeping little boy, who lay beside her in the bed, his head resting against her side.

He sobered. "They found my dad."

She blinked and stared at him. "Was he…?"

"He was in the concrete slab. I knew in my gut Rex was behind his disappearance."

"Oh, Chandler. I'm so sorry."

"Thanks. But I'm good. I knew in my heart—" he hit himself in the chest "—my dad would've come home if he were alive. It's a burden off my shoulders to have closure. I called my mom on the way here."

"How did she take it?"

He smiled. "In true mom fashion. She said, 'Praise the Lord, Simon is home.'" He didn't tell her the part about how his mom had told him how proud she was of him and that his dad would be pleased Chandler had never given up on finding him. He scooted the chair meant for visitors closer to the bed and sat.

Blue eyes stared back at him. The thought of her moving and taking the boy with her was a pang to his heart. He pulled her hand into his and gently gave it a kiss. "I've got a problem."

Her eyebrows came together. "What's wrong?"

"You've talked about picking up stakes and moving again. I don't want you to go." He glanced at the sleeping child and then back to her expectant gaze. "I know we've only spent the last forty-eight hours together, but I don't want it to end."

"What are you saying?"

Dryness attacked his throat, but he needed to say it. Even if she said he was moving too quickly, he had to take the chance. "I love you, Bristol, and I know it's too early to admit, but I'd like to get to know you better."

A smile spread across those beautiful lips, and she threw her arms around his neck. "I think I can handle that."

EPILOGUE

Spencer said, "I'll beat you back to the barn."

"You're on." Bristol nudged the horse and gripped the reins. She stood in the stirrups as Honey galloped toward the barn. Spencer rode Lightning, a paint pony, right in front of her. Mud kicked up from the pony's hooves. Bristol pulled up alongside her son and pumped her arms to give the impression she was trying to go faster. Determination crossed the boy's face, causing her to laugh.

They raced into the yard at the same time.

Tucker barked excitedly, and Chandler wore a smile as he opened the gate for them.

"I won." Spencer's face lit up with joy.

"You sure did."

Chandler took the pony's reins and led him to two square hay bales stacked on top of one another. The height was perfect for the boy to slide out of the saddle. Another bale sat beside the two, and Spencer climbed down without assistance. "You're becoming a superb horseman."

"I'm a cowboy," Spencer corrected. Dressed in his boots, jeans and tractor baseball cap, he played the part well. She couldn't help but smile, as her husband, too, looked good in boots and jeans.

She dismounted, brought her horse to the trough for a drink and let her cool down while Chandler helped with Spencer's horse. The last day of school had been this past Friday, and she'd been waiting for the right time to talk with Chandler. Being a teacher brought its challenges, but with the end of the school year, kindergarten graduation and a slew of extra activities, life had been blissfully busy and satisfying.

Archie Carroll's trial had just finished, and he'd received twenty years in prison for his part in the drug deals and his attack on Josie Hunt. The list recovered from the abandoned batch house provided authorities a map for bringing down a local drug ring. A few of the people weren't convicted, as there was no proof other than being on the list. Josie had fully recovered and was back to working cases to reunite children with their families. Near the grave of Simon Murphy was Mia, Rex's first wife. Her family had had her remains flown back to Italy, her childhood home, for a proper burial.

After Chandler put the gear in the barn, he patted Spencer on the head. "You did good today, son."

A smile spread across Spencer's face. Even though he had been clingy after last year's incident and had struggled with nightmares for a few weeks, with the help of Kennedy Boone, the psychologist with Bring the Children Home Project, he'd gradually returned to his normal carefree self. Bristol wondered how it would affect him in the future, but for now, Spencer was a happy kid.

"Will you go get Tucker a treat from the house?"

Her son beamed up at her. "Sure. Come on, Tuck."

Bristol waited until the duo marched off to the house before wrapping her arm through Chandler's. "I'm glad to be off for the summer. Riding again has been wonderful."

He pulled her close. "You're a natural. But I'm surprised you didn't jump the creek today. Did you chicken out?"

"Are you kidding? You know me better than that." After she and Chandler married last summer, life had been a whirlwind of good things. Spencer had taken to him immediately. They had moved into Chandler's ranch house and bought horses from his mom, since no one rode them much anymore. Sydney turned out to be a doting aunt and built a tiny house on Trudy's property. Chandler's mom had started dating a widower from church a couple of months ago. Chandler said it felt odd to see his mom with someone else, but she had told him no one could ever replace his father. Time would tell what became of that relationship. There was only one thing that could make Bristol's life any more complete.

"Nothing's wrong with Honey, is there?"

"No." She rubbed her belly. "I thought I should put off horse jumping for a few months."

He jerked his head, and his eyes searched hers. "Are you saying what I think you're saying?"

She laughed, and Chandler swooped her into his arms and kissed her soundly. "Chandler Murphy, Spencer is going to be a big brother. I love you."

* * * * *

Dear Reader,

Thank you so much for reading Bristol and Chandler's story.

I can't tell you how much I enjoy writing about the Bring the Children Home team members. I can only imagine what it must be like for families to lose a child—the not-knowing, the searching, the desperation for answers. It's a painful subject.

In real life, there are many organizations that help law agencies find and bring home children. Many are run by volunteers. I pray one day there will no longer be a need for these groups, but until then, thank you and God bless you.

I love to hear from readers! You can connect with me at conniequeenauthor.com or on my Facebook page at facebook.com/queenofheart-throbbingsuspense.

Connie Queen

Get 3 FREE REWARDS!

We'll send you 2 FREE Books plus a FREE Mystery Gift.

FREE Value Over **$20**

Both the **Love Inspired®** and **Love Inspired® Suspense** series feature compelling novels filled with inspirational romance, faith, forgiveness and hope.

YES! Please send me 2 FREE novels from the Love Inspired or Love Inspired Suspense series and my FREE gift (gift is worth about $10 retail). After receiving them, if I don't wish to receive any more books, I can return the shipping statement marked "cancel." If I don't cancel, I will receive 6 brand-new Love Inspired Larger-Print books or Love Inspired Suspense Larger-Print books every month and be billed just $6.49 each in the U.S. or $6.74 each in Canada. That is a savings of at least 16% off the cover price. It's quite a bargain! Shipping and handling is just 50¢ per book in the U.S. and $1.25 per book in Canada.* I understand that accepting the 2 free books and gift places me under no obligation to buy anything. I can always return a shipment and cancel at any time by calling the number below. The free books and gift are mine to keep no matter what I decide.

Choose one: ☐ **Love Inspired Larger-Print** (122/322 BPA GRPA) ☐ **Love Inspired Suspense Larger-Print** (107/307 BPA GRPA) ☐ **Or Try Both!** (122/322 & 107/307 BPA GRRP)

Name (please print)

Address   Apt. #

City   State/Province   Zip/Postal Code

Email: Please check this box ☐ if you would like to receive newsletters and promotional emails from Harlequin Enterprises ULC and its affiliates. You can unsubscribe anytime.

Mail to the Harlequin Reader Service:
IN U.S.A.: P.O. Box 1341, Buffalo, NY 14240-8531
IN CANADA: P.O. Box 603, Fort Erie, Ontario L2A 5X3

Want to try 2 free books from another series? Call 1-800-873-8635 or visit www.ReaderService.com.

---

*Terms and prices subject to change without notice. Prices do not include sales taxes, which will be charged (if applicable) based on your state or country of residence. Canadian residents will be charged applicable taxes. Offer not valid in Quebec. This offer is limited to one order per household. Books received may not be as shown. Not valid for current subscribers to the Love Inspired or Love Inspired Suspense series. All orders subject to approval. Credit or debit balances in a customer's account(s) may be offset by any other outstanding balance owed by or to the customer. Please allow 4 to 6 weeks for delivery. Offer available while quantities last.

Your Privacy—Your information is being collected by Harlequin Enterprises ULC, operating as Harlequin Reader Service. For a complete summary of the information we collect, how we use this information and to whom it is disclosed, please visit our privacy notice located at corporate.harlequin.com/privacy-notice. From time to time we may also exchange your personal information with reputable third parties. If you wish to opt out of this sharing of your personal information, please visit readerservice.com/consumerschoice or call 1-800-873-8635. **Notice to California Residents**—Under California law, you have specific rights to control and access your data. For more information on these rights and how to exercise them, visit corporate.harlequin.com/california-privacy.

LIRLIS23

HARLEQUIN
PLUS

Try the best multimedia subscription service for romance readers like you!

Read, Watch and Play.

Experience the easiest way to get the romance content you crave.

Start your **FREE TRIAL** at
<u>www.harlequinplus.com/freetrial</u>.